'Yo... ...e,' he said.

'Is—is that such a good idea?' she said, her fr... ...er a

'I mean…will there be room for us?'

The look in his eyes was inscrutable, but there was a hint of amusement lurking around his mouth. 'Molly can sleep in her pram and you can sleep in my bed.'

Sabrina's eyes widened, her heart giving that annoying little extra beat again. 'Are you by any chance going to be there too?' she asked, with an attempt at an arch look.

'In my bed, do you mean?'

She nodded, hastily disguising a nervous swallow.

'Only if I am invited,' he said, with a sexy slant of his mouth.

Melanie Milburne says: One of the greatest joys of being a writer is the process of falling in love with the characters and then watching as they fall in love with each other. I am an absolutely hopeless romantic. I fell in love with my husband on our second date, and we even had a secret engagement, so you see it must have been destined for me to be a Harlequin Mills & Boon author! The other great joy of being a romance writer is hearing from readers. You can hear all about the other things I do when I'm not writing, and even drop me a line at: www.melaniemilburne.com.au

Recent titles by the same author:

THE VENADICCI MARRIAGE VENGEANCE
THE FIORENZA FORCED MARRIAGE
THE MARCIANO LOVE-CHILD
INNOCENT WIFE, BABY OF SHAME

The Royal House of Niroli:

SURGEON PRINCE, ORDINARY WIFE
  (Book 2)

Did you know that Melanie also writes for Medical™ Romance?

SINGLE DAD SEEKS A WIFE
  (The Brides of Penhally Bay)
THE SURGEON BOSS'S BRIDE
HER MAN OF HONOUR

Don't miss Melanie Milburne's book
THE FUTURE-KING'S LOVE-CHILD
out in October 2009
part of THE ROYAL HOUSE OF KAREDES

BOUND BY THE MARCOLINI DIAMONDS

BY
MELANIE MILBURNE

MILLS & BOON®
Pure reading pleasure™

First published in Great Britain 2009
Harlequin Mills & Boon Limited,
Eton House, 18-24 Paradise Road, Richmond, Surrey TW9 1SR

© Melanie Milburne 2009

ISBN: 978 0 263 87415 0

Set in Times Roman 10½ on 12¾ pt
01-0809-51922

Printed and bound in Spain
by Litografia Rosés, S.A., Barcelona

BOUND BY
THE MARCOLINI
DIAMONDS

I have often seen books dedicated to editors or agents in the past, and thought—No, I don't need to do that. This is business. But I am afraid I cannot write another book without publicly thanking my current editor, Jenny Hutton, who has been the most amazing support to me both professionally and personally. This one is for you, Jenny, and I hope we get to do many more together. XX

CHAPTER ONE

IT SEEMED like only weeks ago that Sabrina had attended her best friend's wedding, now she was attending her funeral. Any funeral was sad, but a double one had to be the worst, she thought as Laura and her husband Ric's coffins were solemnly carried out of the church by the dark-suited pallbearers.

Sabrina caught the eye of the tallest of the men bearing Ric's coffin, but quickly shifted her gaze, her heart starting and stopping like an old engine. Those coal-black eyes had communicated much more to her than was fitting for a funeral. Even with her head well down, she could still feel the scorch of his gaze on her, the sensitive skin on the back of her neck feeling as if a thousand nerves were dancing with excitement in anticipation of the stroke of his hand, or the burning brush of his sensual lips.

Sabrina cuddled Molly close to her chest and joined the rest of the mourners outside the church, taking some comfort in the fact that at only four months old the little baby would not remember the tragic accident that had taken both her parents from her. Unlike Sabrina, Molly would not remember the sickly sweet smell of the lilies and the sight of the grief-stricken faces, nor would she remember the burial, nor watch in crushing despair as her mother was lowered into the ground, knowing that she was now all alone in the world.

The procession moved to the cemetery, and after a brief but poignant service there the mourners moved on to Laura's stepmother's house for refreshments.

Ingrid Knowles was in her element as the grieving hostess. She brandished a rarely empty glass of wine as she chatted her way through the crowd of mourners, her make-up still intact, every strand of her perfectly coiffed bottle-blonde hair lacquered firmly in place.

Sabrina kept a low profile, hovering in the background to keep Molly from being disturbed by the at-times rowdy chatter. Most of Laura and Ric's close friends had left soon after the service—apart from Mario Marcolini. From the moment he had entered the house he had stood with his back leaning indolently against the wall near the bay window, with a brooding expression on his arrestingly handsome face, not speaking, not drinking…just watching.

Sabrina tried not to look at him, but every now and again her eyes would drift back to him seemingly of their own volition, and, each time they did, she encountered his dark, cynical gaze centred on hers.

She quickly looked away again, her heart skipping a beat and her skin breaking out in a moist wave of heat as she remembered what had happened the last time they had been alone together.

She was almost glad when Molly started to become restless so she could escape to another room to see to the little baby's needs.

When Sabrina came back out a few minutes later, Mario was no longer leaning against the wall. She let out a breath of relief, assuming he had left, when all of a sudden she felt every hair on the back of her neck rise to attention when she felt a hard male body brush against her from behind.

'I did not expect to see you again so soon,' Mario said in his deeply accented, mellifluous voice.

Sabrina took a shaky step forward and slowly turned around, cradling Molly protectively against her breasts. 'No, I…I guess not.' She lowered her eyes from the startling intensity of his dark brown ones, her brain scrambling for something else to say to fill the gaping silence. What was it about this man that made her feel like a nervous schoolgirl instead of a mature woman of twenty-five? He was so sophisticated, so urbane, such a man of the world, and she was so—she hated to say it but it was true—gauche.

'Um, it was very good of you to come all the way back to Australia when you'd only just left,' she mumbled.

'Not at all,' he said in a tone that had a rough, sandpaper sort of quality to it. 'It was the least I could do.'

There was another loaded silence.

Sabrina moistened the parchment of her lips, trying not to look at him, trying not to think of how close he was standing to her, and how foolishly she had reacted to that closeness just a matter of weeks ago. Would she *ever* be able to erase that totally embarrassing—no, mortifying—few minutes from her mind?

'Laura's stepmother seems to be enjoying herself,' Mario commented.

Sabrina met his sardonic, midnight gaze. 'Yes. I'm kind of glad now Laura's father isn't around to see it,' she said. 'Laura would be so embarrassed if…' She bit her lip, unable to speak, fresh tears springing to her eyes as she bowed her head.

She felt a warm and very large hand touch her briefly on the shoulder, the tingling sensation it set off under her skin feeling as if a million bubbles of an effervescent liquid had been injected into her blood.

She brought her gaze back to his once more, a rueful grimace contorting her face. 'I'm sorry,' she said. 'I'm trying to be strong for Molly's sake, but sometimes I just…'

'Do not apologise,' he said in that same deep, gravel-rough tone. He paused for a moment and, lowering his gaze to the sleeping baby in her arms, asked, 'Do you think Molly is aware of what is happening?'

Sabrina looked down at the tiny baby and released a sigh. 'She's only four months old, so it's hard to say. She is feeding and sleeping well, but that's probably because she is used to me looking after her occasionally.'

Another silence tightened the air, tighter, tighter and tighter, until Sabrina could feel the tension building in her throat. She felt like a hand was round her neck, the pressure slowly building and building.

'Is there somewhere we can speak together in private?' Mario asked.

Sabrina felt that same invisible hand suddenly reach inside her and clutch at her insides and squeeze. She had sworn after the last time that she would never allow herself to be alone again with Mario Marcolini. It was too dangerous. The man was a notorious playboy; even in a state of grief he was unable to shake off his air of rakish charm. She felt the warm waves of male interest washing over her even now, those sleep-with-me dark eyes of his sending a shiver of reaction racing up and down her spine every time they came into contact with hers.

Her eyes flicked briefly to his mouth, her stomach knotting

all over again at the thought of how she had been tempted to taste its promise of passion in the past. Her lips had never felt quite the same since, nor had the rest of her body, which had been jammed up against him so tightly she had felt every hard, male ridge of him…

Sabrina gave herself a mental shake. This was hardly the time or place to be thinking of her one and only lapse into stupidity. She squared her shoulders and nodded towards a room off the main living area. 'There's a small study through there,' she said. 'It's where I put Molly's pram and changing bag earlier.'

She led the way, conscious of his gaze on her with every not-quite-steady step she took. No doubt he was comparing her to all the glamorous women he cavorted with back home in Europe, she thought with a kernel of bitterness lodging in her throat. His latest mistress was a catwalk model, tall and reed-slim, with platinum-blonde hair and breasts that would have made sleeping on her stomach uncomfortable if not impossible. But then he had probably moved on to someone else by now. He was known for changing his girlfriends like some people changed their shirts.

It was a lifestyle Sabrina could not relate to at all. The three things she longed for most in life were love, stability and commitment, and she knew she would be nothing but a gullible fool if she thought for even a moment that someone like Mario Marcolini could give them to her. He might be as handsome as sin and as tempting as the devil, but he was way out of her league, and always would be. Her gauche attempt to get him to notice her at Molly's christening had more than confirmed that.

She opened the study door and, moving across to where

the pram was, gently tucked Molly under the pink-bunny rug before turning to face Mario. Yet again she had to fight the urge not to stare at him. He was so impossibly good-looking it was heart-stopping even to glance at him. At six-feet-four, he towered over her five-feet-seven, and with that ink-black, glossy hair and those equally dark, glinting eyes he made her feel mousy and grey in comparison.

He closed the study door with a click that immediately dulled the sound of the chatter and clatter of the wake going on without them. It was like a volume switch suddenly being turned down; it made the silence of the study all the more intimidating, the closer confines of the room making her all too aware of the fact that he only had to take a stride or two to reach out and touch her.

His eyes met hers, holding them as if he had some sort of secret, magnetic power over her; she couldn't look away if she tried. 'We have a problem to solve and it needs to be solved quickly,' he said.

Sabrina paused for a moment to moisten her lips with the tip of her tongue. She had been preparing herself for this, but even so, now that it came to the crunch, she felt devastated. She knew what he was going to do. He was going to take Molly back to Italy with him and there would be nothing she could do to stop him. She would never see her little god-daughter again if the very rich, very powerful and very ruthless Mario Marcolini had anything to do with it.

'You have been informed that we have been appointed joint guardians of Molly, correct?' he said, still watching her with that brooding, hawk-like gaze.

Sabrina nodded, her throat moving up and down over a knot of despair. She had been informed a couple of days ago of the terms of the guardianship Laura and Ric had nominated in their wills. She had also been told it was going to be challenged by Laura's stepmother, who believed she and her new husband could offer Molly the more stable and secure future.

The lawyer had been up front about Sabrina's chances of keeping Molly in her care, and it didn't look good. The court would decide on the basis of the best interests of the child: for instance who had the most to offer in terms of security, of the child's welfare and future provision. Sabrina was not only single, but currently out of work, while Ingrid Knowles and her husband, Stanley, although on the wrong side of fifty, were more than well off and had made no secret of their wish for a child.

'Y-yes,' she said, running her tongue across her chalk-dry lips again. 'I am well aware of Laura and Ric's wishes, but the legal advice I have been given is I stand very little chance of fulfilling them due to, er, my current circumstances.'

He gave her an inscrutable look. 'Your current circumstances being that you are single, unemployed and lately labelled a home-wrecker, correct?'

As much as it galled Sabrina to agree with him, what choice did she have otherwise? The press had made her out to be a bed-hopping babysitter with her eyes on the main chance. She had wanted to defend herself, but knew she could not do so without upsetting the Roebourne children by exposing their father for the perfidious and lecherous creep he was.

'Pretty much,' she said with a grim set to her mouth. 'Laura would be heartbroken to think her stepmother will get custody of Molly. She hated Ingrid with a passion. She told me so only a few days before…' she gulped back her emotion '…before the accident.'

Mario began to slowly pace the room back and forth, like a caged lion meticulously planning an escape. Sabrina stood with her arms crossed over her chest like a shield. She kept her breathing as shallow and steady as she could, but even so she felt her nostrils flare as the exotic spices of his aftershave insinuated their way into her system, making her feel intoxicated, as if she had breathed in a powerful, aromatic drug.

'I will not allow that woman and her husband to have full custody of Ric's child,' Mario said, turning to face her, his dark eyes diamond-hard with determination. 'I will do everything, and I mean *everything*, in my power to prevent it.'

Sabrina felt her heart sink at his adamant statement. This was it. This was the part where he would state his intention of taking Molly back with him to Italy. Her stomach churned with anguish; how could she let this happen? Surely there was something she could do? She had grown up without her mother, without someone who loved her and understood her. How could she let the very same thing happen to little Molly?

'I have a temporary solution,' Mario said.

'Y-you have?' Sabrina's voice was barely audible.

'We are Molly's godparents, and legally appointed guardians. These are both responsibilities I intend to take very seriously.'

'I understand that but, as you say, we are both responsible for her, and I too take those responsibilities equally seriously,' she said, wishing she had sounded more determined and less intimidated. Wishing she *felt* less intimidated.

His eyes held hers for a tense moment. 'Then we shall have to share those responsibilities in the best way we can.'

'What are you suggesting?' Sabrina asked, conscious of a frown tugging at her forehead. 'I live in Australia, you live in

Italy. It's not as if we can share custody of an infant, or at least not in what the courts will acknowledge is an acceptable way with Molly's best interests at heart. She can't be shifted back and forth between countries. She's just a baby, for God's sake. I'm not sure what it's like in your country, but here the courts are big on what is best for the child.'

His jaw was set in an intractable line, his black-brown gaze still drilling into hers. 'Ric was my best friend,' he said. 'I will not stand by and let his daughter be brought up by a couple who in my opinion are not worthy of the custody of an animal, let alone a small infant.'

'All the same, I think it's going to be almost impossible to present a case against Ingrid and Stanley over Molly's custody,' she said, tearing her gaze away from his mouth with an effort. 'I don't know what else I can do. I have looked at this from every angle, and I can't help thinking the odds are against Laura's and Ric's wishes ever being granted.'

There was another silence, weighted with something Sabrina couldn't quite identify. She felt the tension in the air, the humidity of the atmosphere, the pressure of the unknown, the calm before the tumultuous, uncontrollable storm that was stealthily approaching.

'I think we should get married as soon as possible.'

The words fell into the silence like boulders into a calm pond. The rings went outwards, rolling towards her, each one threatening to swamp her. Waves of panic washed over her; she swallowed great, drowning mouthfuls of it before she could speak.

'W-what did you say?' she choked.

He gave her a level look. 'It is the only way we can secure Molly's future,' he said. 'We are her godparents; if we marry, it will convince the court we are the most suitable candidates for her guardianship.'

Sabrina felt her brain start to whirl like an out of control adventure-park ride. Surely she was hearing things; had he *really* just suggested they marry each other? They were practically strangers. They had only met twice, and each time had circled each other like wary opponents. How could she agree to such a preposterous plan?

'Think about it, Sabrina,' he said. 'I am a rich man who can provide everything Molly will ever need. You are an experienced hand at looking after infants and small children. We are also young enough to be good substitute-parents. It is a perfect solution.'

Sabrina finally located her voice, but it came out sounding like a rusty hinge. 'You're asking me to—to *marry* you?'

Mario's eyes flickered in irritation at her tone. 'It will not be a real marriage, if that is what is making you baulk at the prospect,' he said. 'We can each live our own lives—but of course you would have to live with me in Italy, at least until Molly is of an age when she does not need you so much. After that, we can reassess the situation and take appropriate action.'

Her grey eyes blinked at him, her soft mouth falling open, her cheeks developing a faint blush. 'Live with you…in Italy?' she said on a gulp.

Mario felt his annoyance rising at her. He was the one putting himself out on a limb here; he had sworn marriage was something he would never submit to. He loved his freedom; he relished every minute of being his own man, living the life he wanted to live without the ties of a permanent relationship. But, after receiving the news about his best friend's death, he'd realised he would have to step up to the plate, and quickly.

Ric had once risked his own life to save Mario's during a skiing trip in the Swiss Alps when they were nineteen. Mario knew he would not be alive and well today if it hadn't been for Ric's courage and persistence at digging him out of that avalanche with his bare hands. The bond of friendship that had always existed between them, had become so strong after that day Mario had felt sure even way back then that only death would be able to sever it.

Ric had trusted him to see to Molly's interests and he would honour that trust, even if it meant temporarily tying himself to a woman with a more than tarnished reputation. Sabrina Halliday was all demure girl-next-door on the outside, but Mario had tasted a tiny morsel of what was simmering on the inside of that slim but all-woman figure. No doubt that was why she was playing the hard-to-get game with him now. He knew how gold-diggers worked, and as far as he was concerned she was a text-book case. She might have genuine affection for Molly, but that didn't mean she wasn't aware of how much she could gain out of this situation.

'I am prepared to pay you for every year we remain married,' he said. 'I am even prepared to negotiate with the amount.'

The frown she gave him seemed too quick to be anything but genuine, but he was well used to the guiles of women with dollar signs in their eyes.

'You think I want to be *paid* to be your wife?' she asked.

He pinned her grey gaze with his. 'You can have what you want, Sabrina, name your figure. I want Molly under my care and I will pay anything to achieve it.'

This time her face went pale and her small, white teeth

began to gnaw at her bottom lip. 'I think you've got the wrong idea about me—'

'Let's not dawdle any longer over this, Sabrina,' he cut her off impatiently. 'I realise moving to another country is a big step to take—but, with what has been happening here recently, do you not think it is an ideal time to escape from all the innuendo and speculation that has surrounded you?'

Sabrina felt her face crawl with colour. Just like everyone else in Sydney, he thought she was guilty. She could see it in his eyes, the way they ran over her as if he could see right through her clothes. The press hadn't done her any favours, certainly, but surely he of all people knew how the media worked? He had been subjected to it all of his life, so how unfair was it for him to so readily assume she was as she had been portrayed?

But *marry* him?

Her stomach dropped at the thought of being in the same country as him, let alone the same room. He was everything she was not. Hadn't she proved that by her clumsy attempt to kiss him that day? How could she possibly agree to marry him and subject herself to daily temptation? And, even more worrying, would she be able to withstand any attempt on his part to consummate the union if he took it upon himself to do so? He was temptation personified. She could feel the sexual energy of him here and now. Every time his eyes connected with hers it was like being exposed to powerful radiation, making her body hum inside and out.

'You have not found a new position as a live-in nanny, and it is my guess you will not be able to for quite some time,' he continued. 'After all, what self-respecting wife would want to employ a well-known seductress to take care of her children?'

Sabrina ground her teeth. 'I am no such thing. I was used as a scapegoat and no one would believe me.'

His expression was brimful with cynicism. 'It is of no concern to me what you did or who you did it with,' he said. 'I need a wife in a hurry, and as far I can see you are the most suitable candidate.'

She curled her top lip at him. 'I find it surprising you would want a wife with such a track record as mine. Aren't you concerned I will be a bad influence on Molly?'

'I have seen you with Molly, and I do not have any doubts over your love and care for her,' he said. 'Besides, she is used to you handling her, and I do not want her routine disrupted any more than it has been already. I do not know the first thing about babies, and quite frankly nor do any of the women I normally associate with. Plus, it was the wish of Laura and Ric that we should care for Molly.'

Sabrina felt a tiny hook-like tug somewhere in the middle of her chest at the thought of all the women he would continue to see if she married him. 'A marriage of convenience' was the term, a mutual agreement that benefited both parties, this time for the sake of a small, tragically orphaned child. Mario would continue his playboy lifestyle while she would act the role of the long-suffering wife. Oh, she would be well and truly compensated, of that she was sure. Money was no object when it came to the Marcolini bloodline. Upon his father's death a few months ago, Mario had taken over the Marcolini investment business even though he was not the eldest son. His older brother Antonio was a high-profile plastic surgeon who travelled the world lecturing on his ground-breaking techniques for facial reconstruction surgery.

Between the two of them the money they had inherited and earned was beyond anything Sabrina could imagine. When she had lost her mother at the age of ten, the foster family who had taken her in had by no means been on the breadline, but they'd been frugal and conservative with their spending and their lifestyle. Necessities were saved for and purchased, but never luxuries. Sabrina had not even been to a proper restaurant until the age of sixteen, when she had saved up enough money from her various babysitting jobs to go out to celebrate a friend's birthday.

Mario Marcolini on the other hand had probably been fed by five-star chefs all his silver-spooned life. The suit he was wearing looked as if it was a designer label; the silver watch on his tanned wrist probably cost more than her car. Everything about him spoke of wealth and privilege, which was no doubt where he had obtained his air of arrogance. His cleanly shaven jaw had a hint of stubbornness to it, and although she knew from experience how sinfully sensual his mouth could be she suspected it too could be equally intransigent if anyone stood in the way of what he wanted.

The sound of a tiny cry came from the pram, and Sabrina blinked herself out of her stasis to soothe Molly, who was due for a feed and change. 'Hey there, little one,' she cooed as she picked up the little pink bundle. 'What is all the fuss about, hmm? Are you hungry?'

'May I hold her?'

Sabrina turned with the baby in her arms, surprised at how deep and scratchy Mario's voice had sounded. 'Of course,' she said, stepping towards him.

He took the baby carefully from her arms, one of his hands brushing against her breast as he did so. Sabrina tried to disguise her reaction, but she could feel the heat pooling in her cheeks all the same.

She watched as he cradled Molly against his broad chest, his large hands and long, strong forearms making the infant look so small in comparison. A corner of his mouth began to lift in a wistful smile as he looked down at the little girl, one of his long fingers stroking her tiny cheek. *'Ciao, piccolo; sono il vostro nuovo papa,'* he said.

Sabrina found it amazing how one small infant could effect such a change in a man's demeanour. Gone was the cynical glint in his dark gaze; in its place was a tender warmth that made her wish he would look at her like that. She pulled back from her traitorous thoughts, shocked at how she was reacting to him. Perhaps it was his out-of-the-blue proposal that had weakened her normally rigid resolve. Like him, she would do anything to protect Molly, but what he was suggesting made her feel as if she was wading out of her depth into very murky, dangerous water.

Being formally tied to him would mean much more than sharing a house and the care of a child. In spite of his assurance, the marriage would not be a real one. She couldn't help but think living with him over any period of time would blur the boundaries, for her if not for him. From the first moment she had met him at Laura and Ric's wedding eighteen months ago, she had felt a zapping sensation when his deep brown eyes had meshed with hers. It had made every nerve beneath her skin tingle with awareness; her stomach had felt hollow and her legs watery. He had flirted with her outrageously, and yet somehow she had managed to play it cool even though inside she had been simmering with reaction, a reaction she had not been able to control when she had met him again just a few weeks ago. She was not normally the sort of woman to have her head turned with suave good looks. She had always been so guarded around men, which made the fiasco with the Roebournes all the more ridiculously ironic.

There was a sound at the door, and Ingrid Knowles came sweeping in. 'Where is my grandchild?' she asked, her words slurring slightly. 'I want to show her off to some of my friends who have just arrived.'

Sabrina felt her back come up like the fur of a cornered cat. 'Molly needs changing and feeding first,' she said. 'And she is not your grandchild—she is no relation to you whatsoever.'

Ingrid's mouth pulled tight as she gave Sabrina an up-and-down look that had talons attached. 'You think you're going to keep her, don't you? Well, you are not. I have already spoken to my lawyer. You don't stand a chance—not after what you did to poor Imogen Roebourne, seducing her husband behind her back.'

Sabrina felt one of Mario's arms go round her waist, while the other cradled the baby against his broad chest. 'You have been misinformed, Mrs Knowles,' he said with cool authority. 'Sabrina was totally innocent in the Roebourne affair. The press made it out to be something it was not.'

Ingrid gave a grating laugh. 'And you believe her?'

'Yes, I do, actually,' he responded smoothly. 'I would not be marrying her otherwise.'

Ingrid's penciled eyebrows shot upwards. 'You're marrying *her*?' she choked in stunned surprise.

His arm subtly tightened around Sabrina's waist. 'We will be married as soon as it can be arranged and take Molly with us back to Italy.'

Ingrid turned her attention to Sabrina. 'Is this true?' she asked, with a gaze as narrow as a starling's. 'Are you really marrying this man?'

Sabrina felt the seconds ticking by as she hesitated before she answered. The band of Mario's arm was warm about her; she could feel every one of his splayed fingers on her hip, the warmth spreading to her inner thighs like a trail of slow-burning fire. By opening her mouth and agreeing to his plan she knew she was not just stepping onto hot coals but throwing herself into the flames.

Her eyes flicked to where Molly was nestled against Mario's chest, her sweet little doll-like face turned in Sabrina's direction. Her little Cupid's bow mouth smiled as she looked at her, and for Sabrina that clinched it. How could she possibly say no now?

'Um…I…yes,' she said. 'That's right. We're, er, getting married.'

Ingrid gave her another scathing look. 'Then you are an even bigger gold-digger than I thought. You hardly know the man. You've met him—what?—twice? How can you possibly think of marrying him unless it's for money? That's what this is about, isn't it? You've always fancied being the wife of a rich man, and who is richer than a Marcolini?'

Sabrina felt her face suffuse with colour. 'This is not about money.'

'That is correct,' Mario interjected. 'It is about what is best for Molly. It's what her parents wanted for her.'

Ingrid threw Mario a malevolent glare. 'You don't stand a chance. Stanley will engage a top lawyer who will make mincemeat of you.'

Mario's eyes glinted with steely implacability. 'Before he

does that, perhaps you had better tell him I know all about what he has been doing with the Whinstone account.'

There was a throbbing pause.

Sabrina could see how Laura's stepmother was clenching and unclenching her teeth, her green eyes darting about nervously. She almost felt sorry for the woman. For all Ingrid's beverage-fuelled bravado, what chance did she stand with Mario Marcolini as an opponent?

'You're not going to win this,' Ingrid said through thin lips, although her defiant stance had visibly sagged.

Mario's hand tightened possessively on Sabrina's hip as he gave the older woman an imperious smile. 'I believe I just did,' he said. 'Sabrina has agreed to be my wife, and that as far as I am concerned is the end of it.'

No, Sabrina thought with a funny, moth-like fluttering sensation in her stomach as Ingrid stalked out. *It is just the beginning.*

CHAPTER TWO

'YOU DO not need to look so worried, Sabrina,' Mario said as he gently handed Molly over. 'I don't think we will hear from Mrs Knowles again once we are officially married.'

Sabrina busied herself with seeing to the baby's needs rather than meet his eyes. Oh, dear God, what had she committed herself to? There was no way she could wriggle out of this without compromising Molly. Mario had hinted at something untoward in Stanley Knowles's business dealings. And, knowing what Laura had felt about her stepmother and what Sabrina had seen for herself, how could she step aside now to let such people be the guardians of her little god-daughter?

The tiny baby girl cooed at her as if to confirm it, her tiny arms reaching towards Sabrina's face, the little starfish hands touching her on the cheeks, a gurgling chuckle of delight coming out of her rosebud mouth.

'I will arrange for a special license,' Mario said, watching as she leaned forward to press a soft kiss to the middle of each of Molly's tiny palms.

Sabrina continued to dress Molly with hands that were not quite steady. 'How soon do you expect it will be before we…?' She faltered over the word. 'Er, marry?'

'As soon as it can be arranged,' he answered. 'No longer than a week, maybe even less.'

Sabrina felt her stomach lurch sideways. *A week?* She picked up the baby and laid her against her right shoulder as she faced him again. 'That seems…rather rushed.'

'Do you have a current passport?' he asked.

'Yes, but—'

'Good,' he said. 'I will need that and your birth certificate to make all the arrangements.'

'Mario, I—'

'It is imperative we get going on this, Sabrina,' he said with an indomitable look. 'Besides, I want to get back home to where my business commitments await me.'

No doubt your mistress awaits you too, Sabrina thought resentfully as she took out Molly's bottle, which was encased in the Thermos container, and settled down to feed the restless baby. Once Molly was sucking contentedly, Sabrina looked up at Mario who was standing a short distance away, watching her like a predator with its targeted prey.

'You said it wasn't to be a real marriage,' she said, feeling her cheeks bloom with colour, and her whole body shiver in reaction as she thought of what a real marriage to him would involve if he put his mind to it. 'You also intimated it was temporary. What sort of time limit are you thinking of?'

'Molly is a tiny infant,' he said. 'She needs a full-time mother at least until she is of nursery-school age.'

Sabrina felt suspicion crawl up her spine, making her sit more upright in her chair. 'So what happens then?' she asked.

'I will engage the services of a nanny and then you can have your freedom.'

Sabrina frowned at his arrogance. 'So I am to be expelled from Molly's life just like that?' she asked.

'Not necessarily from Molly's life,' he said. 'But from mine. We can have a quiet dissolution of the marriage and then both get on with our lives.'

'So let me get this straight,' she said with a guarded look. 'You get full guardianship of Molly in Italy while I get sent back to Australia, is that what you're suggesting?'

He gave an indifferent lift of one broad shoulder. 'That will be entirely up to you, of course,' he said. 'As my ex-wife you will have full residency in my country, but whether you choose to live in Rome or Sydney will ultimately be your decision.'

'Do you really think I would just walk away from Molly as if she meant nothing to me?' she asked, still frowning furiously. 'And what about what Molly wants? She will have come to look upon me as her mother. She's practically doing it now. What you are suggesting is not just outrageous, it's cruel to both Molly and to me.'

He lifted his dark brows at her vehemence. 'Come now, Sabrina,' he said coolly. 'You have looked after young children before, becoming involved with every aspect of their lives, only to leave when the family no longer requires your services.'

'That's not the same thing at all,' Sabrina argued.

'Are you saying you did not have any affection for the children you were employed to look after?' he asked.

Sabrina could feel her hatred of him simmering in her veins. It was pulsing through the intricate, narrow network in her body, threatening to burst out at any moment. She knew what he was doing; he was going to sideline her right from the start. She would be more than useful to him during the next two or three years while Molly was a baby and toddler, but after that she would be dismissed, just like any other servant in his employ.

'Of course I develop great affection for the children in my care, but Molly is my godchild, the daughter of my best friend. It's an entirely different relationship, especially given the circumstances now.'

'Your marriage to me will not be permanent,' he said. 'As long as you understand that, there will not be a problem if you wish to continue to see Molly once our marriage is brought to an end.'

Sabrina stood and lifted the baby against her chest to wind her, gently patting the tiny back, her eyes still tussling with his. 'You think you've got this all worked out, haven't you? I know what you are doing, Mario. You want a cheap baby-sitter while you continue to live your playboy lifestyle.'

He gave her a smile, his eyes reflecting its mockery. 'Cheap, Sabrina?' he said. 'Is that how you would describe yourself? Certainly the press called you such, and a whole lot more, if I recall.'

She gave him a flinty glare. 'I am not going to be dismissed from Molly's life at your say-so. I want to remain a part of her life no matter what happens between us.'

'Nothing is going to happen between us, Sabrina,' he said. 'Or have you got other ideas, hmm? A little affair with me to pass the time, just like you did with Mr Roebourne, *sì*?'

This time her look was withering. 'I have met some creeps in my time, and up until now Howard Roebourne was at the top of that list. But you, Mario Marcolini, have just bumped him off.'

His smile was still mocking as he came up close and

stroked a long finger down the baby's cheek. Sabrina sucked in a breath; he was so close she could see the sandpapery stubble on his jaw, and the unfathomable black holes of his pupils in the deep, dark chocolate of his eyes. The air around her face carried a trace of his scent, a mixture of aftershave and male pheromones, making her heart give a funny, out-of-time beat.

She quickly lowered her eyes and encountered the flat plane of his chest and stomach; she could almost imagine the six pack of ridged muscle lying beneath his designer shirt. She daren't look any lower; she had spent too many nights as it was thinking about how he was made. The hardened length of him in full arousal as he had taken control of her amateur kiss at Molly's christening had made the blood race frantically in her veins both then and since.

She felt his finger beneath her chin as he lifted her face upwards. 'Is that how you did it?' he asked with a curl of his lip and a hard glint in his eyes. 'Is that how you lured a respectable married man away from his wife, by looking at him with those smoky, grey come-to-bed eyes of yours?'

Sabrina would have pulled away from his touch but she didn't want to disturb Molly, who had drifted off to sleep against her shoulder. 'I did not seduce him, or anyone,' she said, glaring back at him.

His finger moved from beneath her chin and came to her mouth, tracing a pathway over the fullness of her bottom lip, barely touching, making every sensitive nerve begin to leap and dance beneath the skin. 'Ah, but that is not quite true, is it, Sabrina?' he said in a low spine-loosening murmur. 'It is not hard to see why so many men would find it hard to resist a taste of its sweetness. I have not forgotten how tempting it was to taste it myself when you so very kindly offered it to me.'

Sabrina stood very still, barely able to breathe in case she betrayed herself. She wanted to taste his finger, to draw it into her mouth, to suck on it, to see if his pupils would flare with desire the way she suspected hers were currently flaring. Her gaze flicked to his mouth, the sensual contours of it pulling on the secret strings of desire deep and low in her belly. It was like torture to stand so close and not touch him. She had blamed the champagne the day of the christening, but she was stone-cold sober now, and still she wanted his mouth to set hers alight. What was wrong with her? Was she somehow turning into the raunchy Jezebel the press had made her out to be?

His hand dropped from her face. 'I need to get going,' he said, glancing at his watch. 'I will come by your apartment this evening with some papers for you to sign.'

Sabrina could feel the walls of her prison starting to close in on her. When Mario Marcolini wanted something done, he was like a freight train going at full speed. This was the time to say, *no, I won't be a part of this*. Why then wasn't she saying it? The words were on the tip of her tongue, hovering there, but somehow she couldn't utter them out loud. Saying no to Mario would be saying no to Molly; she was sure of it.

He had already demonstrated how ruthless he could be in his dealings with Laura's stepmother earlier. What was to stop him doing the same to her? If she refused to marry him he was quite likely to use her sullied reputation against her. He would apply for full custody of Molly, and with his wealth and status there wouldn't be a judge in the country who wouldn't give it to him. With his pedigree and fortune he had so much to offer a little orphaned child. And Sabrina knew full well if he didn't marry her to secure his claim he would simply marry someone else, and then she would never see

Molly again. She was lucky he had offered her a compromise, although why he had done so was anyone's guess. Stripped down, it was nothing more than blackmail, and yet she had no choice but to agree to the terms. What else could she do? Other women before her had made sacrifices for those they loved. She would do the same.

Sabrina bit her lip as she gently tucked Molly back into the pram. If Mario thought she would be shunted aside some time in the future, he had better rethink his plans. She wasn't going to desert little Molly, no matter what the cost to her personally.

Mario escorted Sabrina out past the other mourners, one or two of them stopping to look in on the sleeping baby, murmuring their condolences; others, like Ingrid and Stanley Knowles, carried on with their drinking and chatting as if they were at a garden party.

Once Molly was safely strapped into the baby carrier in her car, Sabrina turned to look at Mario. 'Do you have my address?' she asked.

'I looked it up in the phone book,' he said. 'I will be round about eight or so.'

Sabrina's gaze flicked back to the house, her brow pleating with worry. 'What if Ingrid comes round before then?' she asked, swinging her gaze back to Mario. 'She's come round each day since Social Services released Molly into my care. The last time she was quite abusive. It was embarrassing for me, not to mention for the neighbours, most of whom are elderly. I was sure someone was going to call the police. I considered doing it myself, except I didn't want the press to get wind of it.'

He drummed his fingers on the roof of her rusty car for a

moment. 'Then it will be best if you and Molly are not there if she should take it upon herself to drop round.'

Sabrina felt another frown pull at her brow. 'But where will we be?'

'You will be at my hotel with me,' he said.

'I-is that such a good idea?' she said, her frown deepening, her heart stuttering in panic. 'I mean…will there be room for us?'

The look in his eyes was inscrutable, but there was a hint of amusement lurking around his mouth. 'Molly can sleep in her pram, and you can sleep in my bed.'

Sabrina's eyes widened, her heart giving that annoying little extra beat again. 'Are you by any chance going to be there too?' she asked with an attempt at an arch look.

'In my bed, do you mean?'

She nodded, hastily disguising a nervous swallow.

'Only if I am invited,' he said with a sexy slant of his mouth.

Sabrina pulled her own mouth into a prim line. 'That is not going to happen.'

'No, of course not,' he said as his smile turned to a sneer. 'You have a taste for the forbidden, do you not? The married man is more your style.'

'I can assure you that all of your married friends will be quite safe from me,' she said with a lift of her chin.

He took her chin between his finger and thumb, his eyes boring into hers. 'I perhaps should remind you at this point of the behaviour I expect from you during the period of our marriage,' he said.

Sabrina considered pulling out of his hold, but, though it was firm enough to make her think twice, it was somehow gentle enough for her not to even want to try. She felt the slow but steady burn of his touch, the heat of him going to her core where a cauldron of need was still on the boil from the last time he had come this close. She ran the tip of her tongue over her lips, her stomach giving a little kick of awareness when he brushed the pad of his thumb over where her tongue had just been. It was like negative meeting positive, fire meeting fuel, flame meeting tinder. She felt her whole body respond; her breasts peaked, her inner thighs trembled and her heart didn't just pick up its pace, it all-out sprinted. 'I—I'm not sure what you expect me to do,' she said, trying to steady her out-of-control breathing. 'It's not as if we are, er, in love or any-thing—and for that matter I am not prepared to pretend we are.'

His eyes continued to hold hers. 'I am glad you mentioned that particular four-letter word,' he said. 'You are more than welcome in my bed, but do not get any ideas about making this arrangement more permanent. I know how a woman's mind works, so any vows of love from you will be disregarded henceforth.'

Sabrina was taken aback by his words. She bristled at his arrogant assumption that she would fall in love with him so readily or, even more insulting, pretend to do so for personal gain. It just went to show the sort of women he sought to warm his bed. He wanted shallow and short term, not deep, caring and committed. 'I could never love someone like you,' she threw back. 'You are the very opposite of what I want in a part-ner.'

He smiled that mocking smile again. 'Is that so?'

She pulled her shoulders back, her eyes flashing their dis-like of him. 'You are selfish, for one thing,' she said. 'And ruthless, and…and…' She hunted for some other words to describe him, but it totally confounded her that all she could think of was how good he was with Molly. For a playboy he certainly was astonishingly at ease around a tiny baby. He handled Molly with care and confidence. He had been the same at the christening, kissing her tiny nose and each of her miniscule fingertips one by one, his normally cynical and hard, black-brown eyes all but melting.

'But I am rich,' he said, still smiling. 'That surely makes up for what else I lack, *sì*?"

'You do not have enough money to tempt me,' Sabrina said with a toss of her head.

'We will see,' he said, and opened the passenger door.

She frowned at him again. 'What are you doing?'

'I am holding the door open for you.'

She rolled her eyes. 'Yes, I can see that, but why? I can't drive it from this side, in case you haven't noticed.'

'I will drive,' he said. 'You can tell me where to go.'

'That will be the easy part,' she said with a pert look. 'Go to hell.'

His dark eyes glinted with amusement. 'Not unless I get to take you with me,' he said. 'I have a feeling we could really ramp up the heat down there with just a kiss or two, let alone the full works.'

Sabrina pressed her lips into a flat line of disdain. 'You don't get to sample the goods, Mario, they're not on offer.' *Not any more*, she mentally tacked on, not entirely sure if it was a promise or a prayer for help in resisting temptation.

'I know what you are doing, Sabrina,' he said. 'You have been doing it from the first moment we met. You like to slowly reel a man in, do you not? That is your modus operandi, no? Little by little you up the ante until he finally capitulates.'

She took a step backwards. 'I am doing no such thing.'

He leaned closer, capturing her chin again, his eyes locking on hers. 'I will take your slim little body any time you like,' he said in a low, spine-tingling drawl. 'Any time, any place, any position. You just have to say the word. Just like the last time.'

Sabrina felt her insides erupt into flames, the hot spurts of need anointing her intimately as she thought of what he would be like as a lover. Inexperienced as she was, she knew enough about him to know he would be everything a woman could want in a sexual partner: demanding, exciting, daring and dangerously attractive. The one kiss they had shared had shown her that and more. It had sent shooting sparks from one end of her body to the other, licking her senses into a frenzy of want. She could feel the pulse of her blood now, hectic and overly excited at his nearness. Her eyes went to his mouth, his fuller lower lip drawing her gaze like an industrial-sized magnet. All she had to do was step up on her tiptoes and their mouths would touch and burn...

The sound of other guests spilling out of the house was the only thing that saved Sabrina from making a total fool of herself all over again. She pulled out of Mario's hold and slipped into the passenger seat, her legs still trembling long after he had stridden around and got in behind the wheel of her four-cylinder car.

Once he was sitting beside her, she suddenly realised how very small her car was. It was like a child's toy; although he pushed back the driver's seat to its maximum distance from the wheel to accommodate his length, every time he worked the gears she was aware of his suited arm within touching distance of her thigh.

'I thought you would have hired some swanky Italian sportscar while you are here,' she said once they were on their way. 'Isn't that what rich men like you do?'

'I saw no need to waste money on one when I was only going to be here for such a short time,' he answered evenly.

Sabrina chewed over that for a moment. 'What if I hadn't agreed to your plan?' she asked, not trusting herself to look at him.

'Then I would have found some way of convincing you,' he said, equally smoothly.

This time she did look at him. 'With blackmail, like you did with Ingrid and Stanley Knowles?'

He met her eyes for a brief moment, before turning back to the traffic. 'I see no reason not to use a bit of pressure when it is warranted,' he said.

Sabrina huddled in her seat, wondering how far he would have gone to make her change her mind if she had said no— not that she'd really had a chance to say no. Ingrid had come in and the words had tumbled out of Sabrina's mouth, words that now tied her to a man she knew so little about.

It was a disturbing thought. All she knew was Mario Marcolini was ruthless in business and equally so in his private life. Women came and went from his life like clouds in the sky, none of them lasting long enough to make an impression on him. She wondered if he had been hurt by a past lover, or if he was just one of those men, all too common these days, who shied away from commitment. All she knew about his background was what Laura had told her in snatches, and, because Sabrina hadn't wanted to sound too curious, she hadn't asked the questions she had longed to know the answers to. Questions she had no right to even be thinking, let alone asking.

'Where to from here?' Mario asked when he came to a crossroads.

'Turn right at the next lights,' she said. 'My flat is in the fourth building on the left, but really I don't think it's such a good idea for me to move into your hotel with—'

She stopped when she saw a news van parked outside her building, the cameras already being set up. 'Oh no…'

'Put your head down and ignore them,' Mario said as he parked the car in the tenants' parking area behind the tired-looking inner-city building. 'I will deal with them while you go in and pack what you need. I can always send someone over later to get the rest.'

Mario fielded the press with a few short statements about his intentions, even embellishing the facts a little for his own amusement. He watched as the news team drove away a few minutes later, and then with a sigh of satisfaction turned and entered the building.

Sabrina's flat was neat and tidy inside, but he could see why she had always sought employment in the upper echelons of society. Like the many gold-diggers he had met or had dealings with in the past, she was obviously looking for a way out of her current situation. A rich man, even if he was married, could set her up as his mistress. Things had backfired on her with Howard Roebourne, but no doubt there would be other rich men once he put an end to their temporary marriage, Mario thought sceptically.

'How long have you lived here?' Mario asked as she came out with a battered suitcase into the tiny lounge area.

'A couple of years,' she said. 'I'd like something bigger and in a nicer suburb, but there's really not much point when most of the families I have worked for have required me to live with them for extended periods.'

'It must at times be difficult to have a private life when you are living with other people,' he said, taking the bag out of her hand and placing it near the door. 'No wonder you have been tempted to work and play under the same roof.'

Her grey eyes flashed as they hit his. 'You think I'm a slut, don't you? And yet the papers are full of your sexual exploits. Your double standards make me sick.'

'I have not resorted to sleeping with married women,' he said. 'I have plenty of single and unattached ones to work my way through first.'

She swung away from him, snatching up her handbag and hoisting it over her shoulder. 'I suppose you have a revolving door on your bedroom?' she said, flashing him another glare.

Mario grinned at the thought. 'Not yet, but it sounds like a great idea,' he said.

Her glare intensified. 'I think you are disgusting,' she spat. 'You have no morals. You probably don't even spare the women you bed with another thought once you have done with them. It's such a shallow and selfish way to live.'

'It is no more shallow and selfish than touching what does not belong to you,' he pointed out.

'You know nothing about me,' she said with a mulish jut of her chin as tears welled up in her eyes. 'You think you do, but you don't.'

He pushed himself away from the door frame where he had been leaning. 'I know what Howard Roebourne told me about you.'

Sabrina felt her face drain of colour as her heart began to pound sickeningly. 'H-how do you know him?' she asked.

'The business world is not as big as you might think,' he answered. 'Roebourne and I move in the same financial circles. I happened to run into him at a corporate function when I was here the last time.'

'W-what did he say?' she asked, even though she wasn't sure she really wanted to know. After that last horrible scene with her previous employer, she could not think of a single thing he could say that would paint her in an attractive light.

'Nothing I had not already worked out for myself,' he said with an enigmatic smile.

Sabrina silently ground her teeth. So *that* was why he had allowed her to kiss him on the day of Molly's christening, to see if what he had heard about her was true. Her shameless grasp at him hadn't done her any favours, she realised now when it was far too late to do anything to change things. If he had only suspected she was a wanton woman before, her behaviour at the christening would have been more than enough confirmation that his suspicions were accurate. She had acted so out of character that day. She had blamed the three glasses of champagne she had consumed, but she had only drunk them out of sheer nervousness in his presence.

It had started the day of the wedding when he had captured her gaze and held it. Something had passed between them that day, something visceral. And then at the christening it had been activated all over again by Mario's debonair charm, his lethally attractive smile, and the sensual glide of his hand on her bare arm as he had taken the baby from her. She had felt it as soon as his eyes had locked with hers, drawing her to him, holding her, making her burn for him as if he had turned on a switch inside her body. Try as she might, she hadn't been able to locate it since and turn it off. She had felt that same tingle of awareness even when his name had been mentioned, let alone standing in his presence as she was doing now.

'Are you ready to leave?' he asked as he picked up Molly in the baby carrier in one hand and her old suitcase in the other.

'Yes,' she said, avoiding his eyes.

Once Molly was back in the car and the suitcase stowed, Mario got back behind the wheel. 'I suppose I should warn you that the press will go wild about our forthcoming marriage,' he said. 'I know you are not keen on the idea, but I think the best approach is to let everyone believe this is a genuine love-match. That is what I told them back there at your flat. They seemed to be delighted by it.'

Sabrina stared at him in wide-eyed alarm. 'You told them I was *in love* with you?'

He grinned at her wickedly. 'Of course I did. I have my reputation to maintain, don't forget. I can't have people thinking you married me for my money. It's demeaning.'

'But I am only marrying you because of Molly, and it was your choice to pay me,' she pointed out wryly.

He gave a shrug of indifference. 'Yes, but no one else needs to know that. Have you decided how much you want?'

Sabrina swallowed tightly as she turned to look out of the passenger window. There was no amount of money on this earth that would ever bring her best friend back, but if she could put any of the money Mario gave her into an investment account for Molly it would be something. When Sabrina's mother had died, she had been left with nothing. The stigma of being penniless and at the mercy of others' charity had never left her, even after all these years. Of course Molly, being under Mario's protection, would want for nothing, but Sabrina wanted to demonstrate her commitment to her god-child by herself providing her with a nest egg when she came of age. She was determined not to touch a penny of it for herself.

'I can almost hear the ching-ching of the cash register in your brain,' Mario said. 'You are doing the sums, calculating how much you will need to set yourself up for life.'

She sent him a spiteful glance. 'I want half a million for every year we are married.'

'In Australian dollars or euros?' he asked without flinching.

Sabrina tried to recall the current exchange-rate. 'Um…in euros,' she said, wishing she had asked for more just to annoy him.

'If you give me your details, I will make sure the first in-stalment is in there once we are married.'

Sabrina toyed with the strap of her handbag for a moment. 'You said earlier you expected me to take your name,' she said, pausing to glance at him again. 'Is that really necessary in this day and age?'

'Sabrina Marcolini,' he drawled. 'Now that has rather a nice ring to it, does it not?'

She pursed her lips. 'I prefer Halliday. It was my mother's maiden name.'

'You don't have a father?'

'Not that I know of,' she said, fiddling with her handbag strap again. 'My mother never mentioned him. I think he might have been married or something. She seemed reluctant to give me any details. I found a photo once, but when I asked who it was she scrunched it up and I never saw it again.'

There was a momentary silence.

'You said it *was* your mother's name,' he said. 'Does that mean she has since married again?'

'No, it means she is dead,' Sabrina said, stripping her voice of the aching emotion she still felt. 'She died when I was ten. The train she was travelling to work on was derailed. She was the last to be pulled out of the wreckage.'

'I am very sorry,' he said. 'Neither Ric nor Laura ever mentioned it to me.'

'Laura understood how hard it was to grow up without a mother,' she said. 'She lost hers when she was a little older than I was, but when her father married Ingrid only weeks later she was totally devastated. She felt she had lost both of her parents right then and there. Her father died just before she met Ric…but I suppose you know all this?'

He shifted the gears, a frown stitching his brow. 'I did not really know Laura all that well,' he said. 'I only met her for the first time at the wedding, where, if you remember, I also met you. Ric and I went to elementary school together. We remained in close contact even when his family emigrated to Australia when he was fourteen.'

'Did you ever visit him?'

'Yes, I have been to Australia seven times now, and Ric came back to Italy on holidays occasionally,' he said. 'My brother was here in Sydney just a couple of months ago.'

'Yes, I read about it in the paper,' Sabrina said. 'I saw the name and assumed it was your brother. He was here for a lecturing tour, wasn't he?'

'Yes, but also to sort things out with his estranged wife.'

Sabrina felt her brows lift up in intrigue. 'Oh?'

He changed the gears again. 'They were living apart for five years but they are back together now,' he said. 'They renewed their vows only a few weeks ago. They are expecting a child in a few months.'

'Are you pleased about their reconciliation?' she asked, watching his expression for a moment.

'I am very happy for them both,' he answered after a pause. 'I might not be a family man, but I recognise when a couple belong together. There was a time however when I thought Antonio would have been better off moving on without Claire, but I am prepared to admit I was wrong.'

'I don't think it is wise to take sides in a marital dispute,' Sabrina said, thinking of all the times Laura had let off steam about Ric's hot-headed stubbornness, only to be madly in love with him the next moment.

As the silence stretched Sabrina couldn't help feeling Mario's brother's situation explained a lot about his cynical attitude towards relationships. He had seen his brother go through a lengthy estrangement. There was no way he was going to give any woman in his life the same opportunity to put his life on hold. His relationships were on his terms and his terms only. Love didn't come into it, nor did permanency, even when there was a child involved.

Mario needed her now to act as a substitute mother to Molly, but she was on borrowed time, and if she had any hope of coming out of this with her heart intact she had better keep reminding herself of it.

This is not for ever.

This is not for real.

She took a mental gulp and added: *this is dangerous.*

CHAPTER THREE

THE hotel Mario was staying in was exactly where Sabrina had expected someone of his ilk to stay: top-end luxury, panoramic harbour views, several five-star restaurants, as well as a piano bar and an in-house gym, and a health spa which was second to none in terms of decadent indulgence. His penthouse suite was superbly decorated with the latest in high-street trends, the modern open-plan design making it feel more like a mansion than a hotel apartment.

The views from every window were breathtaking, even for someone who had lived in Sydney all of her life, Sabrina conceded. The harbour was dotted with colourful yachts and the bustle of passenger ferries criss-crossing the sparkling waters to take commuters and tourists wherever they needed to go.

Molly was still sleeping in her carrier, which gave Sabrina time to unpack a few things into the spacious wardrobe Mario had told her she was to use during their short stay.

However, she resolutely turned her back on the massive king-size bed made up in a thousand threads of Egyptian cotton, with numerous feather pillows, and a doona that looked as if it was filled with air. But even so she couldn't help thinking of Mario lying there, possibly naked; yes, she decided, he would *definitely* be a naked sleeper, his long, tanned limbs splayed out in any number of erotic poses.

She gave herself a stern mental shake and concentrated on the job at hand. She had a tiny baby to settle into yet another routine, and in a few days a long-haul flight to another country, a country where she knew only the basics of communication, in spite of Laura's giggling tutorage over the last few months.

It struck Sabrina again, then, how surreal the last few days had been. Laura, the one friend who had understood her passion for connection and belonging, was gone, never to return. She kept thinking someone was going to shake her awake and tell her it was all a mistake, that the bodies taken from the wreckage of Ric's car were not those of him and Laura but someone else, strangers, no one she knew—no one she loved so dearly and would miss for the rest of her life.

Just like the day her mother had died, Sabrina was alone again... Well, not quite alone. She had Molly, dear, precious little Molly, who was thankfully oblivious to what had passed in the last few days. There would be a day when she would need to be told the truth about her real parents. Sabrina could only hope she would be around to tell Molly what a wonderful and loving mother Laura had been, how much she had loved her baby and had wanted the best for her, leaving her in the care of the two people she had trusted most in the world: her husband's best friend and hers.

How ironic that those two people hated each other, even though they both loved the child, Sabrina thought as she folded another pink baby-suit and laid it on the shelf.

The baby gave a grizzling sound, and Sabrina went over

to her, scooping her out of the carrier and cuddling her close, breathing in that sweet infant smell, her hand cupping the black down of that tiny, silky head. 'Shh, my precious,' she said softly. 'I know this is all new to you. It's all new to me too. We'll have to take one day at a time until I can think of a way out of this.'

Mario heard Sabrina's voice just as he came to the door of the bedroom. So she was thinking of an escape route, was she? Not while he had anything to do about it, he determined. She would likely face a kidnap charge if she left without consulting him as co-guardian.

Ric's wife had had nothing but good to say about her friend, but that didn't mean Sabrina hadn't personally woven the wool she had pulled over Laura's eyes. Mario had to admit Sabrina had an innocent look about her that was beguiling to say the least. Ric had obviously fallen for it too; he had told Mario at the wedding how delightful Sabrina was, how charming, how unworldly, shy and self-effacing, even dropping broad hints about what a suitable partner she would make for him. Mario had laughed off the suggestion; he had met plenty of supposedly shy women in the past and in his experience they were the ones who turned out to be the most devious and coolly calculating. It was the quiet ones you had to watch.

And he had been right about Sabrina. His interesting little conversation with Howard Roebourne the evening before Molly's christening had confirmed what a go-getter Sabrina was behind that sweet girl-next-door exterior. The woman who had thrown herself into his arms for those few stolen moments had been hot and hungry, her mouth like an open fire, her tongue a flame that had scorched his, branding him with an imprint he had not been able to erase. He could still taste the sweet temptation of her cushioned lips, the way they had moulded so perfectly to his. Their passionate clinch had been interrupted before he'd been able to take things any further, but he was in no doubt he could have had her then and there. In fact, he was in little doubt he could have her any time he wanted to if he put his mind to it. He saw the way she looked at him with those smoky-grey eyes of hers, the sensual need in them unmistakable.

Mario entered the bedroom and Sabrina turned to face him, the baby cuddled close to her chest. 'Have you everything you need?' he asked.

'Yes,' she said, lowering her eyes to concentrate on tucking in the label of Molly's baby-suit at her tiny neck. 'Everything's…lovely.'

'I have to pick up some legal documents but I should be back within an hour,' he said. 'Make yourself at home. If you want anything for yourself or Molly, call room-service and charge it to me.'

Sabrina hadn't realised she had been holding her breath until he left, the door of the penthouse closing firmly on his exit. The air in the room seemed to lose its tightness once he had gone; her chest felt less restricted, and her heart rate not so hectic.

Molly seemed restless and, although Sabrina had fed her, she decided a warm bath might help the little baby to relax. She carried her through to the *en suite* where twin bowl-like basins were set on top of a highly polished marble bench. She half-filled one basin with warm water and squirted in some baby-bath liquid. Once she had Molly undressed and splashing delightedly in the basin, the little girl's giggles replaced her grizzles. It was times like these that made Sabrina wonder if she would ever have a baby of her own some day. Being tied to Mario for the next three or four years was hardly going to improve her chances of finding a partner.

He on the other hand would no doubt continue his numerous affairs, leaving her to hold the baby, so to speak. The way he had orchestrated things meant he was always going to be in control. But then that was the sort of man he was; he was nobody's lackey, he was as alpha as they came. It still surprised her how much he wanted Molly, however. It just didn't fit with her knowledge of him as the playboy the press made him out to be. Bouncing a blonde bombshell on his knee rather than a baby was more his thing, but then perhaps he was not interested in fathering his own offspring and was content to have the responsibility for a small child's upbringing instead. There was no doubt he cared for Molly, but then how many people could resist a cute, gummy smile and big china-blue eyes?

Once Molly was dried and dressed and, after a cuddle, back in her pram and sleeping peacefully, Sabrina sat on one of the plush leather sofas and flicked through the hotel entertainment and facilities guide, trying not to think too much about the night ahead.

The door opened and Mario came in with a briefcase in one hand. He placed it on the coffee table in front of her, clicking it open and retrieving a sheaf of papers.

'You had better read through these before the lawyer joins us,' he said. 'He's meeting us here in a few minutes. He is still downstairs. He had to take a call from another client.'

Sabrina took the thick pile of paperwork and began reading. It was wordy, as legal documents generally were, but she plodded her way through it, realising that in signing it she was relinquishing the right to any of Mario's assets acquired prior to their marriage. Pre-nuptial agreements didn't sit well with her on principle. She'd always reasoned that if a couple was truly committed to making their marriage work there would be no need for a back-up plan. But then, this marriage was hardly what anyone could call a romantic union. It was little more than a business transaction, and for that reason she decided there was no point in making a fuss about signing on the dotted line. She didn't want Mario's money; all she wanted was for Molly to have a secure and loving home.

The lawyer arrived and after brief introductions he went through the document with Sabrina and indicated where she was to sign.

'That's it,' the lawyer said once the last space had received Sabrina's signature. 'I will speak to the accountant about having an allowance deposited into your bank account, as per Mario's instructions.'

Sabrina felt a tide of colour slowly ebb into her cheeks. She wondered just how much the lawyer had been told about the circumstances between Mario and herself. She was being paid to be a wife to him on paper only, and substitute mother to Molly, and yet as far as she could tell there was nothing in the lawyer's expression that suggested he thought their relationship was anything other than normal. But then perhaps Mario had lied to him as he had done to the press earlier—for the sake of his own reputation, certainly not hers.

Once the lawyer had left, Mario began to tug at his tie. 'I thought I might do a few laps of the pool,' he said. 'You can join me, if you like.'

Sabrina gave him a testy look. 'We have the custody of a baby, remember? You can continue to have your freedom, but

I for one am taking my responsibilities seriously where Molly is concerned.'

His eyes collided with hers. 'Are you suggesting I am not taking my responsibilities seriously?'

She folded her arms across her body. 'Let's be right up-front about this, Mario. You hardly have to do a thing where Molly is concerned. That's why you've got me, isn't it? Your life can continue without interruption while I am left to look after the baby.'

His tie hung loosely around his neck as he came up close. 'Forgive me if I am wrong, but I thought your chosen career was to care for babies and small children?' he said. 'Or are you being particularly bitchy because you do not like the fact that I have prevented you from getting your hands on my fortune when our marriage is eventually terminated?'

She glared up at him, desperately wanting to step backwards, but forcing herself to stand her ground. 'Everything is always about money to you, isn't it? You think I want anything from *you*? I hate you. I can't believe Laura agreed to nominate you in her will as Molly's guardian. In fact, I can't even believe Ric suggested it, since he knew you longer than Laura ever did. He of all people should have known how unfit for the task you are. I have never met a more unsuitable father figure in my life.'

His dark eyes hardened to smouldering black coals of contempt. 'You are a fine one to talk, Sabrina Halliday. You have the morals of an alley cat in heat, opening your legs for the highest bidder.'

Her eyes flashed with pure venom, her whole body quaking with rage. 'At the risk of repeating myself—you are disgusting.'

He stepped closer, so close she had to flatten her spine

against the wall. 'How about if I *were* to make a bid for you, hmm?' he asked in a slow, sexy drawl. 'One that your greedy little hands will not be able to resist?'

Sabrina felt the valves of her heart tighten as his warm breath skated over her face. Her breathing became even more ragged; her legs felt like dampened paper, barely able to keep her upright. 'No amount of money would tempt me to sleep with you,' she said, flashing him a feisty glare.

'Oh, I do not want you to be asleep when we come together,' he said with a sinfully sexy smile. 'Far from it. I want you writhing and convulsing and panting beneath me. That is what you want too, is it not, Sabrina? That is what you have wanted from the first moment we met.'

Sabrina had never felt such an explosion of heat erupt in her face or in her body before. His words, his incendiary, carnal words, had set off fires all through her, each one singeing her like a burning ember pressed to her skin. Images of their bodies locked together in passion flooded her brain, shockingly erotic images that were disturbing, not because she didn't want them to happen but—God help her—because she did.

Denial was her only defence, and as hastily assembled defences went hers was about as unstable as any could be. 'You are mistaken,' she said in a voice that was not quite as steady and controlled as she had hoped. 'I have no interest whatsoever in becoming another notch on your belt.'

He picked up a few strands of her hair, coiling them like a silky rope around two of his fingers, his eyes still burning down into hers. 'It is early days, *la mio piccolo* seductress,' he said. 'We are not yet married; perhaps when you have my ring on your finger and your body in my bed you will change your mind.'

'Don't hold your breath,' she said, still glaring at him, her heart beating like a hyperactive jackhammer.

He gave her hair a gentle tug, pulling her inexorably closer to the hard ridge of his body. Sabrina felt her breath skid to a halt in her chest, her body set alight by the arrantly male and primal probe of his.

The atmosphere tightened; the air around them was brooding, dangerous, and suddenly full of irresistible temptation.

Sabrina felt each 'thud, thud, thud' of her heart like a swinging anvil against her chest, her insides quivering at the brooding intensity of his dark gaze as it held hers. She moistened her lips—discreetly, she had thought—but his gaze flicked downwards, the thick screen of his dark lashes giving him a heavy-lidded, sexy look that sent every thought in her head scattering like startled sparrows.

'I could have you right now, Sabrina, and you damn well know it,' he said in a low, deep tone, his warm, hint-of-mint breath caressing her lips.

Sabrina's gaze was mesmerised by his mouth. Those firm lips were tilted in a smile that promised mind-zapping passion, and her lips tingled in response, aching for the pressure of his. All she had to do was stand up on tiptoe to close the gap between their bodies, like she had that first time. His fire would melt her ice with one brush of that commandeering mouth of his on hers.

Just in time she felt the undertow of commonsense tugging at her, pulling her back from temptation. Oh, she wanted him all right, but that would be feeding right into his cynical opinion of her as a good-time girl after a fast buck and an even faster tumble in his bed.

With the sort of strength she had no idea she possessed,

she pulled out of his hold. 'I don't think so,' she said, mentally berating herself for not sounding as determined as she had planned. The trouble was she didn't know if it was possible to resist him. She was fighting herself more than him, and wondered if he knew it. Desires and needs she had never felt before shuddered through her almost constantly in his presence. Her body felt hijacked, hijacked by a need to be possessed by his hot, hard heat. The heat she could still feel on her skin even though she had put some distance between their bodies.

He waited a beat before asking, 'If it is not more money that you want, what exactly is it?'

Sabrina turned away. 'I realise you are used to having whatever you want, but I am not for sale.'

'Every woman is for sale,' he countered cynically.

'Not this woman,' she said, turning to face him again, her chin up.

The smile playing about his mouth was sardonic. 'We will see.'

'I mean it, Mario,' she insisted.

He rocked back on his heels, his eyes still holding hers. 'Do you ever think about that kiss?' he asked.

She schooled her features into indifference, although her mouth was tingling at the mere mention of that mind-blowing moment when she had tasted his mouth. 'What kiss?'

His smile deepened the grooves either side of his mouth, making him look even more devastatingly attractive. 'You know what kiss.'

'Oh, that.' She waved her hand dismissively. 'I forgot all about it. I was drunk. I can barely remember what I did that day.'

His dark eyes glinted. 'Liar. You remember every last detail, don't you? And you were not drunk—a little tipsy, perhaps, but definitely not drunk.'

She pulled back her shoulders. 'I was not in control of my behaviour that day, and for that I am deeply ashamed,' she said. 'I promise you, it won't happen again.'

'You had better be able to control your behaviour in future, Sabrina, for during the time you are in my bed I expect it to be an exclusive arrangement.'

Sabrina gave him a glowering look. 'Are you usually so confident in the face of rejection?'

His glinting gaze teased hers. 'Always.'

'Then this time you are heading for disappointment,' she said, wondering if she was tempting fate by sounding so confident when she was anything but. He was so potently attractive; every pore of his strong, male body promised an explosive passion. One kiss had shown her how weak her defences were. Hating him clearly wasn't a big enough barrier, for she knew if he took it upon himself to capture her mouth right now she would be lost within seconds.

'If you would like to stretch your legs, I can mind Molly for an hour if you tell me what I need to do if she wakes up,' he offered after a moment.

Sabrina met his dark eyes. She wished she knew what was going on behind that enigmatic expression of his. Was he sizing her up, calculating how long it would be before she capitulated to his advances? Did he know how seriously tempted she was? How could he tell what sort of turmoil her body was going through? Was she giving off some secret signal or something?

'It's all right,' she said, shifting her eyes just out of reach of his. 'Her routine is a little out of sorts just now. She might not wake at all, or she might wake as soon as she hears the door opening and closing.'

He pulled his loose tie away from his neck, coiling it as he stood before her. 'When we get to Italy I can engage a part-time nanny for the times you feel you need a break,' he said. 'There will be the occasional function we will be expected to attend as husband and wife, so we will need the services of a nanny in any case.'

Husband and wife.

Oh, how casually he said those words, Sabrina thought with a savage twist of her insides. They meant nothing to him; they were just words. They did not signify for him the relationship as it was meant to be, the relationship she had longed for all her life—one of closeness, security and friendship. Her mother had been denied it and now Sabrina was suffering the same fate. Life was cruel.

'I would also like Molly to learn my language,' he added. 'It is important she hears you speak it as well as me.'

'But I am not qualified to teach her,' Sabrina said, frowning at him in agitation. 'I can only speak a few words of Italian. I can barely say please and thank you. I'm afraid I don't have much of a talent for languages.'

'I will organise some tuition for you,' he said. 'It is impera-tive that young children hear both languages from an early age in order to become bilingual.'

Sabrina shrugged her acquiescence, even though she knew he would be wasting both his money and the tutor's time. 'As you wish, but don't say I didn't warn you.'

'I would also like you to update your wardrobe,' he con-tinued. 'I will make sure you are well funded to do so.'

Pride stiffened Sabrina's spine. 'There is nothing wrong with my wardrobe as it is,' she said. 'I like my clothes.'

'In my opinion you would look better without them,' Mario teased.

Colour burned in her cheeks as she tried to stare him down. 'You haven't seen, and nor will you see, me without them,' she said. 'That is not part of the deal.'

His eyes roved over her, scorching her, making her feel as if she was standing in nothing but her goose-bumped skin. 'We could always make it part of the deal,' he said, locking his searing gaze on hers. 'How about it, Sabrina? How about another five-hundred-thousand euros to warm my bed?'

Sabrina felt her legs loosen and fought to stand firm. 'N-no,' she said, annoyed that her voice sounded so thready.

He undid the buttons on his shirt. 'If you change your mind, let me know.'

She tried not to stare as his masculine chest was revealed: dark, springy hair, tanned skin, sculptured pectoral muscles and a stomach that was flat and rock-hard. She felt her mouth go dry as she forced her eyes back to his smiling ones. 'What do you think you are doing?' she asked.

'I am getting undressed.'

'Here?' The word came out like a tiny squeak.

'Where else do you suggest I do so?' he asked. "This is *my* hotel room, is it not?'

Sabrina set her mouth into a prim line. 'Yes, but—'

He unhooked his belt. 'I could always do it in the corridor, but then the manager or other guests might have something to say about that, *sì?'*

'I am sure there are changing rooms on the pool deck,' she said, swallowing as he heeled himself out of his shoes.

'Yes, I suppose there are.'

She spun away when she heard the rasp of his zipper. 'Do you mind?' she choked.

'Sabrina, we are going to be officially married within days,' he said.

She hunched her shoulders, keeping her back turned. Did he have to keep reminding her? She was having enough trouble dealing with the reality of being tied to him, without him figuratively hitting her over the head with it at every opportunity. Was he doing it on purpose to show how he had all the power and control? 'So?' she said in a tone that asked 'what does that have to do with anything?'

'So you will have to get used to seeing me without clothes. I do not want my staff to think I have an unwilling wife in my bed.'

Sabrina felt her consternation increasing. 'You said it wasn't going to be a real marriage,' she said hollowly, still with her back turned towards him, every vertebrae feeling as if it was being unhinged as she listened to the rustle of his clothes being dispensed with.

'Nevertheless, we will have to share a bedroom from time to time.'

She spun back to face him, her heart pounding in her chest. 'What?'

'I have dependable, trustworthy household staff at my villa in Rome, but when we stay abroad I must insist we share a bedroom like any other married couple,' he said, folding his trousers over the back of a chair. 'I do not wish the press to make a laughing stock out of me for not having a normal relationship with my wife.'

Sabrina stared at him in rising alarm, her heart rate soaring. 'But…but can't we have separate beds at such times?'

'No.'

Something about his intractable tone annoyed her beyond measure. 'You think I am going to sleep with you without a fight?' she asked, still trying not to look below his waist. He was still wearing his underwear, but with one involuntary glance she had seen enough to make her body crawl all over with traitorous desire.

'I expect you to know which side of your bread is buttered and how thickly, Sabrina,' he returned. 'I am paying you to act as my wife, and that is what you will do when I need you to do it.'

'I am not sharing a bed with you and that is final,' she said with a glittering glare.

'Then I will have to think of a way to convince you to do so,' he said. 'Leave it with me. I am sure I will come up with something.'

Sabrina was immeasurably annoyed that he was so confident she would cave in just like every other woman in his life had before. She was even more annoyed because she suspected he was going to succeed with her in spite of her paltry attempts to hold him off. 'How?' she asked with a curl of her lip. 'By using blackmail?'

His eyes held hers with steely purpose. 'If necessary.'

She drew in a wobbly breath. She was in no doubt of his ruthlessness. He had a hard edge to him that for some inexplicable reason was part of his lethal charm. He was aloof, untouchable, in control and powerful at all times and under all circumstances. 'I hardly think you could say anything about me that hasn't already been said,' she pointed out. 'My reputation is hardly pristine and worth protecting.'

'I was not thinking about using the threat of exposure to the press as my tool,' he said. 'As you say, what would be the point? Everybody already knows what sort of woman you are.'

Sabrina ground her teeth. Oh, how she wished she could prove him wrong. He would not look down at her in that imperious manner of his then. What would he say if she were to tell him the truth—that he wasn't marrying a sleep-around slut but a totally inexperienced virgin?

He would laugh at her, that was what he would do, she reminded herself. It was hardly something you could prove one way or the other, or at least not these days when women were physically active from a young age. It would be her word against her reputation, hardly a level playing-field, given what the press had said about her from day one of the Roebourne affair.

'Not going to deny it?' he asked in the throbbing silence.

'What would be the point?' she asked in return. 'You have already made up your mind about me.'

He held her gaze for endless seconds. 'You are rather a surprise package, Sabrina Halliday. Behind that demure façade you pack quite a sensual punch. I am almost tempted to refresh my memory of how passionate and tempting that soft mouth of yours can be.'

Sabrina stepped backwards, her heart giving a little skip and trip of alarm. 'Don't even think about it.'

He smiled an indolent smile that creased up the corners of his eyes. 'Oh, I am thinking about it, Sabrina,' he assured her. 'I think about it all the time.'

Panic beat a rapid tattoo in her chest as he stepped

closer. 'S-stop it, Mario,' she said a little desperately. 'Stop flirting with me. That's what started it, you know—you flirted with me non-stop at the wedding. Don't do it. It…it annoys me.'

'Do you know what I have been thinking?' he asked as if she hadn't spoken, his dark eyes holding hers like headlights aimed on a frightened fawn.

'No,' she said, running the tip of her tongue over her lips. 'No, I do not want to know what you've been think—'

'I have been thinking about how it would feel to have that soft mouth around me, your tongue licking me, until I—'

Sabrina pressed her fingers against his firm lips to stop him from going any further. 'No, don't say it,' she said hoarsely.

His eyes continued to burn their way into hers as he pushed his tongue against the pads of her fingers, the erotic action sending zigzags of electric heat right to her toes and back.

She pulled her hand away as if it had been burnt, her chest going up and down as she tried to control her erratic breathing.

'We could have fun together, Sabrina,' he said, still holding her gaze. 'Lots and lots of fun.'

She pursed her lips, trying her best to sound firm. 'I would rather watch paint fade…I mean dry.'

He laughed, the deep, rich sound having much the same effect on her as his tongue had against her fingertips. 'It will be interesting to see if that holds true once we are legally married,' he said, reaching for his bathrobe.

'You think putting a ring on my finger is going to suddenly make me find you irresistible?' Sabrina asked with a scowl.

'Diamonds have usually done the trick with all the women I have known,' he said with a mocking smile. 'Did you know

I have recently acquired an investment in a large diamond company?'

She shook her head. 'No, but that's of no interest to—'

'I will have a ring made up with Marcolini diamonds, and then we will see just how irresistible I am, shall we?' he carried on in that arrogant manner of his.

Sabrina was steadily fuming. 'You really have an appalling opinion of women, don't you?'

'I am a realist,' he said, tying the ends of the bathrobe around his waist. 'I know the games women like you play. Money and prestige are paramount. You do not let feelings get in the way of position and power. That would ruin everything, would it not? You didn't love Howard Roebourne, for instance. He was just a meal ticket, a means to an end. What a pity it all went sour for you.'

Sabrina tightened her mouth even further. 'You don't know what you are talking about,' she said.

His dark eyes hardened with cynicism. 'He's told me what you were like, Sabrina. From your activities so far, I have no reason to doubt him.'

Colour flowed into Sabrina's cheeks. She had been so naïve in her handling of Howard Roebourne. She had not recognised the subtle moves he had been making on her until it was too late. 'He was lying,' she said through clenched teeth.

Mario picked up his room card from the table. 'After I have a swim I will have dinner brought up to the suite,' he said. 'That is, unless you think Molly is not too young to be taken out to a restaurant.'

Sabrina pressed her lips together. Dinner with others around would certainly be less threatening than sharing a meal in the room, commodious and luxurious as it was. But then Molly was only four months old, and the clatter of crockery and cutlery would hardly be conducive for a restful sleep. 'Um…I think today has been rather a big day for her,' she said at last.

His eyes held hers for a second longer than she felt comfortable with. 'As you wish,' he said.

Sabrina waited until he had left the suite before she let out her breath in a ragged stream. 'What were you thinking, Laura?' she whispered hollowly. 'For God's sake, what were you and Ric thinking?'

CHAPTER FOUR

SABRINA was sitting on one of the plush leather sofas, flicking through a magazine, when Mario returned from the pool. In spite of every attempt to ignore him, she felt her eyes drawn to his tall, imposing frame. He was wearing the hotel bathrobe but it was now hanging open to reveal the close-fitting black bathers that shaped his male form lovingly. The long, strong, tanned muscular length of his legs made her breath suddenly hitch in her throat. He was so intensely male she seriously wondered if any other man could hold a candle to him without it being snuffed out in shame. His slicked-back hair revealed the handsome contours of his face: his high, intelligent forehead, his patrician nose, his devil-may-care mouth and his dark eyes fringed with thick, black lashes still spiky with moisture from the pool.

'I'm going to have a shower,' he said with a glinting smile. 'Would you like to come in and scrub my back for me?'

Sabrina rolled her eyes and returned to her magazine. 'No thank you.'

'Afraid you might enjoy it?' he asked.

She closed the magazine and gave him a reprimanding

adult-to-recalcitrant-child look. 'Do you *ever* think about anything else besides having your physical desires met?'

His eyes locked with hers in a challenging duel. 'Yes, I do, as a matter of fact,' he answered. 'I think about how you slept with Roebourne under his wife's nose.'

Sabrina stood up and tossed the magazine down with a slap of glossy paper on marble. 'I did nothing with him,' she bit out.

One of his dark brows lifted in derision. 'I just can't quite believe you, Sabrina. I wonder, how much did he pay you to say that?' he asked.

'Have you ever considered I might actually be telling the truth?' she asked with a jut of her chin.

His eyes scanned her face for long seconds, as if making up his mind about her. Sabrina hated that she had a propensity to blush and fidget when under pressure. It made her look guilty and ill at ease, the opposite of what she wanted to convey. But then from the first moment she had been introduced to him Mario had made her feel like a naughty schoolgirl meeting the headmaster for some supposed misdemeanour.

'I have found in life there is not often smoke without some sort of heat behind it,' he said. 'The rumours that stick are usually the ones that have a grain of truth in them.'

'It seems to me it doesn't matter what I say, as you have already made up your mind about me,' Sabrina said. 'I would have thought someone who has spent most of his adult life subjected to the speculation of the press would have realised how unjust that is.'

'Ah, yes, but you have consistently refused to speak to the press,' he said. 'If you had nothing to hide, why not tell your own side of the story?'

Sabrina folded her arms against her chest as an image of Teddy and Amelia Roebourne came into her mind. Their young innocence was worth protecting even if it meant compromising herself. 'I don't have to explain anything to anyone,' she said. 'What I do or don't do in my private life is my own business and no one else's.'

'What you do once we are husband and wife will be very *much* my business,' he said, with a thread of steel underpinning his statement. 'I am sure I do not need to remind you, I am a high-profile businessman with many important clients across the globe. I do not want any personal scandals to disrupt my life, or indeed that of Molly's.'

Sabrina bristled at his autocratic stance. 'I suppose you want me to have no life at all while you carry on as normal? That's called a double standard, Mario, and in this country women don't take too kindly to it.'

'Then it is just as well you will not be in this country but in mine,' he returned. 'Of course, if you don't want to go through with the arrangement I can always find someone else to take up the position.'

Sabrina reined in her temper with an effort. She was dancing on thin ice with him, and he was ruthlessly reminding her of it. He didn't need her half as much as she needed him. The chances of her finding a husband at short notice were very slim indeed; the chances of finding a man who would love and protect Molly as if she was his own were even slimmer. She would have to see this arrangement through, no matter what the cost. There would be compensations, surely. She would have loads of time to be with Molly, to be the best substitute mother possible. And living in a foreign country would be an adventure of sorts. She had often toyed with the idea of working abroad and this was a perfect chance to do so.

'I am not going to desert Molly,' she said, with a determined set to her mouth.

His mouth was tilted in its usual mocking angle. 'Not to mention turn your back on a truckload of money. That would go against everything written in the gold-digger's guide to amassing a fortune, would it not?'

Sabrina glowered at him. 'I can see why your relationships only last a few weeks. No woman in her right mind would put up with your arrogance and rudeness any longer than that.'

'On the contrary, I make a point of always being the one to bring a liaison to an end,' he said.

'Have you ever been in love?' she asked.

'No.'

She couldn't quite stop her lip from curling. 'So your relationships are basically about sex.'

'More or less,' he said with another indolent smile.

Sabrina felt a faint shiver pass over her as his dark eyes held hers. There was something about him that deeply unnerved her when he looked at her like that. It was as if he knew what she was thinking, how her mind was conjuring up images of him pleasuring her, kissing her senseless, crushing her beneath him as he plunged into her moist softness.

She felt her womb contract as his gaze went to her mouth, each and every one of the pulsing seconds swollen with erotic promise. Her tongue darted out to moisten her lips, her heart thundering in her chest as he brushed the pad of his thumb where her tongue had just been, the caress so intimate, so sensually stirring, she felt her lips tingle all over with need.

She wanted to feel his mouth on hers, to taste his maleness, to feel the rasp of his unshaven jaw against her skin, to thread her fingers through his silky black hair, to feel his hard body pressed against hers in mutual longing. She tipped up her face, her eyes half-closed in silent appeal, a soft whimper of need sounding at the back of her throat as his head slowly came down towards hers.

Molly's cry from the bedroom was soft but it was enough to break the spell. Sabrina stepped backwards, one of her hands shakily brushing back her hair, her eyes slipping out of reach of his. 'I—I think she needs changing,' she mumbled as she slipped away.

As she saw to the baby's needs, Sabrina remonstrated with herself for being so foolish as to be tempted by Mario's touch. She had been so close to losing her head. She had been a whisker away from begging him to kiss her. Was she so pathetically weak? She had always been so sensible and in control, but for some reason Mario Marcolini made her feel out of control and reckless. He awakened in her a side of her personality she hadn't known existed. He made her aware of her body in a way no one else had ever done. He had only to look at her and she felt as if her skin had been set alight. Her body pulsed with longing, a persistent ache, that tortured her whenever he was around. It was like an itch she couldn't reach to scratch, a hunger she couldn't satisfy.

Sabrina could hear the shower running as she came back out to the lounge area with Molly in her arms. She tried not to think of Mario's naked body standing under the fine needles of spray, but her mind played traitor all the same. Even after she heard the water being turned off, she began to picture him drying himself with one of the big fluffy white towels.

'Oh, for God's sake,' she chastised herself after a few more minutes of mental torture. 'This must stop.'

'Everything all right?' Mario asked as he sauntered in with a towel slung low around his hips.

Sabrina swallowed tightly as her eyes ran over him. 'Er…yes. Fine…' she stammered.

He came over and tickled Molly under the chin. *'Come è la mia bambina?'* he asked.

Sabrina felt her nostrils flare to take in the clean, sharp tang of his aftershave. He was standing so close she felt his body heat; she could even see tiny droplets of water clinging to his slicked-back hair. He was smiling down at the baby, his eyes like melted chocolate, and his finger now stroking the tiny, dimpled cheek.

'She is so young and defenceless,' he said, meeting Sabrina's gaze.

'Um, yes. Yes, she is,' she said, scarcely able to breathe.

The baby grasped his finger with her tiny hands and gurled at him, her little legs kicking up and down in excitement.

'Is she hungry?' he asked. 'She seems to want to gnaw on my finger.'

'She might be teething,' Sabrina said. 'Some babies get them earlier than others.'

'Does it hurt?' he asked, looking at her again.

Sabrina felt herself drowning in the dark pools of his eyes. His forehead was creased slightly, his expression serious and concerned. 'Sometimes,' she said. 'Their gums can get a little red and sore just before the tooth breaks through.'

His gaze shifted back to the baby in her arms. 'Can I have my finger back, *mio piccolo*?' he asked.

Molly smiled and kicked her legs some more, still clutching his finger with her little dimpled hands.

Sabrina watched as his mouth curved upwards in another smile, the effect on her making her feel as if someone was slowly pulling a long silk ribbon out of her insides. She could see why Ric had insisted Mario be appointed as Molly's guardian. He might be an out and out playboy, but there was no question over his attachment to the child. She had seen biological fathers show less affection for their children than Mario did towards Molly.

Mario gently freed his finger and stroked the baby's wispy dark hair. 'Have you thought about what Molly should call us?' he asked.

Sabrina captured her bottom lip for a moment. 'I'm not sure,' she said. 'Mummy and Daddy seems—I don't know—not quite right under the circumstances.'

'Yes,' he said, frowning slightly. 'I have been thinking the same, but I suppose that is because it has been such a shock. We are not used to thinking of ourselves as her parents. I think in time I will get used to her calling me Papa. I don't want her to address me as "Uncle" or by my first name. I want her to look upon me as her father, even though I am not.'

Sabrina couldn't help noticing he didn't offer any suggestions over what she should allow Molly to call her. She could only suppose it was because he didn't envisage her being around in the long term. She looked down at the baby in her arms and felt her heart tighten at the thought of being shunted aside some time in the future. She couldn't let it happen, even if it meant fighting him tooth and ten bitten nails every step of the way.

Mario stepped back once Molly released his finger. 'Have you decided what you want from the room-service menu?' he asked Sabrina.

'I haven't had time to look,' she said, transferring Molly to her shoulder and gently patting her on the back to soothe her.

He picked up the hotel services guide and handed it to her. 'The chef will do anything to order if there is nothing on the menu that takes your fancy,' he said. 'Help yourself to a drink from the bar while I get dressed.'

Sabrina glanced at the bar once he had left the room, but in the end she decided against a unit or two of Dutch courage. The intimacy of sharing a suite was doing enough damage to her equilibrium. She was already having trouble keeping her mind focussed and in control. The last thing she needed was to have her inhibition blurred by alcohol, given what had happened the last time she had indulged.

Mario came out a few minutes later dressed in black trousers and a casual light blue shirt. His hair was still damp and finger-combed back, giving him a rakish look that was disturbingly attractive. 'Is Molly asleep?' he asked, looking at the baby snuggled peacefully against her neck.

'Yes; I was just waiting for you to come out so I could put her back down,' Sabrina said, moving past him towards the bedroom he had just vacated.

Once she had left, Mario poured himself a drink and wandered over to the bank of windows to look at the view. The city and harbour lights twinkled in the spring evening air, and he watched as a train crossed the Harbour Bridge like a long, golden centipede.

He felt a pang of loss deep in his gut at the thought of never seeing Ric Costelli again. How many times had they shared a drink and chatted about their lives and interests? When he'd received the news of the accident he had been rocked to the core. He had thought it was a mistake, a sick joke someone was playing on him. How could someone so vital and alive like Ric be lying now in a cold, dark grave?

Memories came flooding back: the childhood pranks he and Ric had got up to when they'd been in elementary school; the day Ric had left with his family to come to Australia; the various trips they had taken when Mario had flown over to visit, most especially the skiing, when they had both stared mortality in the face and won.

Mario remembered Ric phoning him two years ago to tell him he had fallen in love with an Australian woman called Laura, and then just four months ago calling him in the middle of the night to tell him he was the father of a baby girl. Now Molly was an orphan; she would never know her mother or her father, never hear their voices, never look into their eyes and see the love they had had for her.

Mario was determined to do the right thing by Molly, even though it meant sacrificing his freedom for the time being at least. Although, the more he thought about it, it might not be such a hardship being temporarily tied to Sabrina Halliday. She had a certain allure about her—that defiant grey gaze, that stubborn chin, that quick-firing tongue and that slim but feminine-in-all-the-right-places body stirred him more than he had thought possible. She certainly wasn't his usual type. But he could not remember a time when he had wanted a woman more. Was it because she had held him at arm's length thus far? It wouldn't be for long, of that he was sure. She was as on-fire for him as he was for her; he could feel it every time their eyes met. It was like a vibration in the air, a high frequency of energy that passed between them. He saw the way her pupils flared, the way her tongue swept over her lips, making them moist and soft and so very tempting to taste.

God, he was getting hard just thinking about it. She would be dynamite in bed; he could tell from the way she had come on to him at the christening. Her soft, full mouth had barely touched his before it had flowered open beneath the responding pressure of his. Her tongue had tangled with his, her small, white teeth nipping at his bottom lip until he had been close to losing control. Her body had been so tightly clamped against his he had felt every delicious contour of hers, and he hadn't been able to wait to have her naked in his arms, to feel her creamy, satin skin against his. He had been tempted to take her up against the nearest wall, but the sound of someone coming had prevented him taking things that far. His body had throbbed and ached for hours afterwards, and he'd determined then that one day, somehow, he would have her.

He would make her forget all about Howard Roebourne and any of her other lovers. It would be *his* name she gasped when she came, it would be *his* bed she occupied, no one else's.

Mario turned and looked at her when she came back into the room. She met his gaze and he felt another surge of blood in his groin.

Yes, she would be *his*, he determined, and he had a feeling it would be sooner rather than later.

'Can I get you a drink, Sabrina?' he asked.

She shook her head. 'No, thank you.'

He twirled the contents of his glass as he held her gaze. 'I can order some champagne, if you would like it.'

A rosy hue came into her cheeks and she shifted her eyes away from his, although her voice was curt. 'No, thank you.'

'Have you decided what you would like to order?' he asked.

Her teeth worried her bottom lip as she flicked through the menu. 'I'll just have some soup and a roll,' she said, briefly meeting his gaze.

He raised one brow in a teasing arc. 'Surely you need more than that to satisfy you?' he said. 'You strike me as a woman of—shall we say—robust appetites.'

Sabrina felt her face grow hot at his *double entendre*. 'No, on the contrary, I am not one for over indulging,' she said, forcing herself to hold his satirical look.

He smiled a knowing smile. 'Only when you think you can get away with it, right?'

She set her mouth. 'Are we talking about food…or something else?' she asked.

'If Roebourne is to be believed, you are insatiable,' he said, still idly twirling the spirits in his glass. 'He said he had trouble keeping up with you.'

Sabrina silently ground her teeth. She could just imagine the light she had been painted in, one that made her look like a predatory trollop with no regard for anyone but herself. However, instead of defending herself, this time out of a perverse desire to annoy him she fed right into his assumptions with her response. 'I am surprised he admitted his failings in that regard. Don't all men like to portray themselves as full-blooded studs no matter what their age?'

A brittle look came into his eyes as they held hers. 'What did you see in him besides his money, I wonder?' he asked. 'He's at least thirty or forty kilograms overweight and as ugly as a hatful, as the saying goes.'

'Unlike men, who place a high value on looks, women are much more accommodating when it comes to choosing a lover,' Sabrina clipped back. 'We choose a mate on other criteria.'

'Money being the primary one,' he inserted with a curl of his lip.

Sabrina gave her head a little toss. 'I am the first to admit that money is not everything, but it does show a man who is going somewhere. No woman wants to be tied to someone who can't enhance her life in some way. What would be the point?'

'What about love?' he asked.

She raised her brow. 'Love, Mario?' Her tone was just shy of scoffing. 'I thought you didn't believe in love. I thought for men like you it was all about the physical, that you would never allow emotions to have a foothold.'

'Just because I have not felt love for a sexual partner does not mean I am incapable of ever feeling such an emotion,' he countered. 'The point is I have not met anyone who has that effect on me as yet.'

'What happens if you were to meet such a woman during the period of our marriage?' Sabrina asked, trying to ignore the strange, tight little ache she felt in her chest.

He put his glass down on the nearest surface before returning his eyes to hers. 'That would indeed be a difficult situation to be in,' he admitted. 'I have made a commitment to Molly, and yet I do not think Ric or Laura would have wanted me to sacrifice my own happiness indefinitely.'

'What if *I* meet someone?' she asked, deciding to play devil's advocate.

The hardness in his eyes turned to black marble. 'I would expect you to do the right thing by Molly,' he said. 'We both have to make some sacrifices until she is of an age where she can understand the circumstances of her life.'

'It's easier for you as a man,' Sabrina said. 'You can hold

off having children of your own for years and years to come. I am twenty-five years old. I don't want to have children in my mid-to-late thirties. I would have liked to settle down in the next couple of years and have children while I am young and fit and healthy.'

'I understand that, and that is why this marriage between us is a temporary arrangement,' he said. 'By the time Molly is of school age, you will still be young enough to get on with your life.'

Sabrina frowned at him. 'But I've already told you, I can't just walk away from Molly like that. And what if the woman you eventually fall in love with resents having someone else's child to bring up? I know of several friends who have had to deal with stepmothers or stepfathers who made their lives absolutely miserable, especially when they have their own biological children. They always felt like the odd one out, like they didn't belong.'

'I will do my best to ensure Molly never feels like that,' he said. 'In any case, I do not envisage falling in love with a woman who does not also love Molly. As far as I am concerned, that child is a part of my life now and will be until the day I die.'

'It's very commendable of you, Mario, but life doesn't always work out the way you think it will,' she said. 'Love isn't something you can switch on and off. It happens, and it can happen between people who are totally unsuitable in other ways.'

'I am not planning on complicating my life in such a way,' he said. 'For the time being my life will continue as it has done. I work hard and I play even harder.'

'Will you be discreet with your playing hard, or am I to

constantly be made a fool of?' Sabrina asked with an excoriating look.

'That, of course, is entirely up to you,' he said with an arcane smile.

She eyed him suspiciously. 'What do you mean?'

His dark gaze ran over her lazily, slowly undressing her as each second throbbed past. 'I would have no reason to make a fool of you by playing around if you were willing to entertain me at home.'

Sabrina felt her spine tingle at his indecent proposal, even though the rational part of her brain baulked at what he was suggesting. 'You think I would agree to be used by you?' she asked.

'For a price, I think you would do just about anything,' he responded cynically.

'I think you need to extend your social circle,' she said crisply. 'You have obviously been mixing with people who are not representative of how normal and decent people behave.'

'Come now, Sabrina,' he chided her. 'You can hardly describe yourself as normal and decent after what you have done. You have been accused of tearing apart a loving family for a roll in the sack with a man almost old enough to be your father.'

Sabrina mentally counted to ten. *Think of the children*, she told herself. It was not their fault they had a sleaze of a father and a cold and vindictive mother. 'In spite of what you might think, I am quite choosy in whom I sleep with,' she said. 'And you, I am afraid, do not qualify.'

Before she could move to counteract it, he suddenly pulled her up against him with such force the breath was knocked right out of her. She felt every hard ridge of him against her;

his belt-buckle dug into her almost painfully, his fingers on her upper arms were like steel clamps and his eyes were like black diamonds as they clashed with hers. 'You are doing this deliberately, are you not?' he ground out savagely. 'Teasing and taunting me with this touch-me-not game. There is of course a rather coarse name for a woman like you. Do I need to remind you of it?'

Sabrina pulled back against his grip but it was impossible to gain any leverage. She felt fear climb up her spine on long, spidery legs, her heart picking up its pace and her mouth going completely dry. 'Y-you're hurting me,' she gasped, even though it wasn't quite true. Her traitorous body wasn't feeling pain; it was feeling desire, hot and strong. The blood was thundering through her veins, making her breathless. Her breasts were swelling, her belly turning to liquid, and her legs trembling as his strong ones bracketed them either side. She felt the bulge of his erection swelling against her, the erotic reminder of all that had pulsed between them from the moment they had first met.

He wanted her.

She wanted him.

And in spite everything she felt about him Sabrina suspected it might not be too long until they both got what they wanted.

'You would open your legs right here and now if the price was right. But I am not going to pay you any more than I have already agreed on.'

'I don't want your filthy money,' she spat at him, eyes blazing with hatred.

'But you want me,' he said, his fingers tightening a fraction. 'I can see it in your eyes and I can feel it in your body.

When we do it, Sabrina, you will not forget it in a hurry, I can assure you. Your body will hum and throb for days afterwards—I guarantee it.'

Sabrina felt her head spin at his sensual promise. She could feel his potency, the dangerous heat of him burning its way through her paltry resistance. She was in no doubt making love with him would be totally unforgettable. One stolen kiss had shown her how vulnerable she was to him. She had practically melted in his arms, just like she was doing now. He had only to bring his mouth down to hers now and she would be his willing slave. It galled her to think she was so weak where he was concerned. What was wrong with her? Was she turning into the sensual witch he took her for?

'Admit it, damn you,' he continued in the same rough tone. 'You want me to beg like all the others have done. That is how you get off, is it not? You like to have power over the men in your life. That way, you can get what you want from them.'

Sabrina was way out of her depth, but doing her best to struggle to the surface. 'You are wrong, Mario,' she said somewhat shakily. 'I don't want any such thing.'

'So innocent,' he said with the customary cynical twist to his mouth. 'Even Ric fell for it, and he was usually so adept at identifying a fraud.'

'I am not a fraud,' she said. 'I am just like you—trying to do the best thing for Molly under incredibly difficult circumstances.'

He put her from him almost roughly. 'I have no idea why Ric and Laura nominated you as co-guardian,' he said. 'But I swear to God, if you put one foot wrong you will never see that child again. Do you understand?'

Sabrina held her ground but on legs that were trembling.

'You can't take her away from me,' she said in a voice that was nowhere near as strong and determined as she had intended.

His eyes burned like a laser beam into hers. 'You just watch me.'

CHAPTER FIVE

SABRINA made herself scarce until their room-service order arrived. Her stomach was in knots of tension and she wondered if she would be able to do the light meal justice with Mario sitting opposite her looking at her in that contemptuous way of his. The injustice of it all was stinging. She had nothing to be ashamed of, other than her blindness to the devious ways of men like her previous employer. If only she had suspected Howard Roebourne's motives from the start she could have done something to prevent the shame of being labelled as the seductress who had shattered the harmony of a supposedly loving family. Imogen Roebourne had latched on to Sabrina as the culprit, not for a moment listening to her denials of any wrongdoing. Imogen had been determined to switch the anger she should have been feeling towards her wandering husband on to the babysitter instead. Sabrina still cringed when she thought of how poorly she had been portrayed in the press. She was almost grateful now she had no living relatives to witness the shame that had been dumped on her. Her foster parents now lived interstate, and rarely kept in touch, but if they were to hear of the rumours Sabrina knew they would automatically assume she was the guilty party.

Sabrina's mother had been a young single-mother in the days when it had still been a stigma to have no man claiming paternity of the child. Sabrina had never known who her father was in spite of her longing to do so, especially since her mother's death. The sense of not belonging to anyone by blood made her longing for a family of her own all the more intense. From a very young age she had dreamed of building a relationship with a reliable and faithful man, bearing his children and raising them in a home that was happy, loving and secure.

Her hopes and dreams would have to be shelved now, for she could see no way how she could abandon Molly—and, attractive as he was, Mario was not the sort of man to settle down and agree to provide Molly with a stepbrother or sister or two. He was intent on doing the right thing by Molly, certainly, but only as far as it didn't interfere with his easygoing playboy lifestyle. That was where Sabrina came in. She would be the wife on paper, the substitute mother, until he found someone more suitable to occupy his bed. Whether or not his future bride if he chose to have one would also occupy his heart was not something Sabrina could decide. It was hard to imagine Mario Marcolini falling in love. He didn't seem the type to allow himself to be vulnerable to anyone. There was an element of the bad boy about him, a fast-living playboy who was untameable in every possible way. And the way he had orchestrated everything so far made her realise how seriously outclassed she was in dealing with him.

But, while Mario was wild and worldly, Sabrina on the other hand desperately wanted to find someone who would love her and protect her—someone who would be there for her no matter what, the sort of man who would look at her with love shining in his eyes, adoring her for who she was, not for how she looked. Not that her looks were anything to be ashamed of. She knew she was fortunate to have inherited her mother's slim figure and model-like cheekbones. Her grey eyes were thickly fringed with dark lashes that hardly needed the boost of mascara, and her skin was fine and clear apart from a light dusting of freckles on her nose.

But men like Mario Marcolini wanted perfection in their partners, and she was hardly that. She didn't possess anything glamourous in her wardrobe, which he had already alluded to; nor did she have expensive make-up in her cosmetic bag, nor did she wear handmade designer shoes. She was a chain-store girl out of necessity, not choice, although she knew how to highlight her best features when the situation called for it. No wonder Mario thought she was trash, she thought. Men born to privilege could be appalling snobs when it came to mingling with the other half, and she was very definitely the bottom end of the other half.

The room-service attendant arrived with a loaded trolley, the aroma of delicately prepared cuisine stimulating Sabrina's flagging appetite.

Mario tipped the attendant, and once the door closed after the young man's exit Sabrina felt the intimacy of the set-up all over again. She was alone in the luxury suite with him, a delicious meal set before them with no possibility of interruptions by other guests or staff like there would be in a restaurant. A bottle of wine was on ice, the scene set for seduction if he put his mind to it.

She chanced a glance at him, trying to read his expression. She felt that tiny quiver in her belly when her eyes met his, the rumble deep inside like a miniature earthquake, reminding her of how much he affected her. Those dark brown, almost black eyes of his contained both cynicism and something else that she suspected was a glint of determination. He wanted to conquer her, to show her to be the wanton woman he thought she was.

The trouble was Sabrina thought he might very well be right. She felt wanton and out of control when in his presence. It wasn't just his debonair looks and worldly charm; it was something else she couldn't quite put her finger on. She wanted to toss caution to one side and experience the passion he promised in every taut and muscular line of his body. As lovers went, she suspected he would be right up there on the scale of demanding, adventurous and earth-shatteringly satisfying. He would expect full participation and do everything possible to achieve it. Her intimate muscles contracted in delight at the thought of experiencing his sensual attentions. She suspected her body would shatter into a thousand pieces of pleasure under the expert touch of his mouth, hands and very male body.

She had seen enough of him so far to know he was not lacking in that department. He wore his sensual expertise like a second skin; she could feel it whenever he touched her. Just minutes ago when he'd had her rammed tightly against him she had felt the power and potency of him, the need building in him to subdue her, to claim her, to make her his in the most primitive and yet natural way possible. Her body recognised him as her nemesis. He was the one man she had no resistance to. She turned into putty when he touched her.

It frightened her to think she had no defences to hold him off. That one kiss four weeks ago still taunted her. She had thought of nothing else since. Her mouth even now was tingling with the need to feel the commandeering pressure of his, to feel his thrusting, searching tongue conquering hers. She had seen how powerfully he was made; she had felt him swollen and erect against her. His dynamic male body would totally consume her smaller one, stretching her, making her a woman in the real sense of the word, showing her a world of feeling that was way beyond what she had experimented with so far.

She had been kissed before, but not with the heated passion Mario's mouth offered. He made every kiss she had ever received seem like a chaste peck on the cheek in comparison. After that first move of hers, he had plundered her with a ruthlessness that had shocked and delighted her at the same time. He had triggered a response in her that she had not been able to damp down since. It was simmering there, keeping the network of nerves under her skin in semi-arousal mode, actively waiting for the next caress, the next touch, that would activate them into hot, throbbing life again.

Sabrina knew she had to be extra vigilant around him. He was too practised at this. He had women all over the globe falling over to experience his possession. She would lose valuable ground in joining them. She had never been one for jumping into the fire; unlike many other women her age, she could delay gratification. It was more or less her hallmark. For all of her adult life she had ignored the advances of men to keep her goals in sight. She wanted more for her life than a temporary liaison that had the potential for heartbreak, as her mother had experienced. And as far as Sabrina could tell Mario Marcolini had 'heartbreak' written all over him. God knew how many women he had already cast aside with their hearts in tatters. She certainly didn't want to be one of them.

'Take a seat,' Mario said as he lifted each of the silver dome-lids covering their meals on the trolley.

Sabrina sat on the edge of her chair, her tastebuds responding to the array of dishes set before her. The delicious-smelling cream-of-mushroom soup and the crusty bread-roll with its shell-like curl of fresh butter made her empty stomach rumble hollowly.

Mario had ordered a man-size meal: tender fillet wagyu-steak, steamed vegetables and a potato dish that was creamy and crispy at the same time.

He poured her a glass of chilled white wine and a glass of red for himself. 'Does Molly usually sleep through the night?' he asked as he picked up his glass of ruby-red wine.

Sabrina picked up her own glass, wondering if it was wise to indulge when she was already teetering on the edge of losing her self-control. 'The last couple of nights she hasn't woken, but usually by about three or four months most babies get into a routine of sleeping through the night,' she said.

Mario spread his napkin across his lap. 'How did you get into nannying?' he asked. 'Was it something you always aspired to?'

Sabrina put down her untouched glass of wine and picked up her water glass instead. 'I have always loved children. I was an only child, so I guess that might have had something to do with it. I worked in a childcare facility for a while, but I felt I wanted to bond with the children, and it was not always possible to do that when kids came and went so often. Becoming a nanny and spending extended periods of time with infants and small children in their own home was much more satisfying for me. I could really get to know them and their routines, as well as become part of the family unit. That in itself is very beneficial for very young children. Of course, no one else could ever replace their mother and father, but having another caregiver who is involved in every aspect of their lives is tremendously comforting to them—especially when both parents are busy professionals and very often time-poor.'

'So how did you come to work for the Roebournes?' he asked with an unreadable look.

Sabrina felt her colour start to rise. Looking back, she could see how stupid she had been in accepting the post. There was no way she could frame it without it sounding as if she had inveigled her way into the Roebourne household in order to conduct a clandestine affair with Imogen's husband.

She switched glasses and took a deep sip of her wine, hoping it would settle her nerves—but all it did was demonstrate how shaky her hand was, a sign of guilt if ever there was one, or so she thought by the way Mario's dark gaze zoned in on it like a hawk swooping down on unsuspecting prey.

She took an uneven breath and, bringing her gaze back to his, explained, 'I met Howard Roebourne at a charity event I was attending. He mentioned his wife was hoping to return to work after staying at home with their two children, who were four and six. He also mentioned how their attempts to find a suitable nanny had failed to find anyone remotely suitable.'

'You were unemployed at the time?' he asked, still watching her with that piercing gaze.

Sabrina tried not to fidget under his scrutiny. 'The family I had previously been working for had recently accepted a posting abroad. I would have gone with them if they had offered me the position, but the children were of school age by then, and the mother decided she wanted be a stay-at-home wife for a change. So, yes, I was at a bit of a loose end at the time.'

'Did you get on with Roebourne's wife?' Mario asked after another short pause.

Sabrina had never been all that good at lying and had to rely on every scrap of acting ability she possessed to answer his question. 'She was always very professional towards me.'

'But you were not friends…' It was neither a question nor a statement, but something in between.

'I was an employee,' she said, becoming increasingly annoyed by his attitude. 'Are you best friends with all the people who work for you?'

'Some I consider friends,' he answered. 'But obviously Mrs Roebourne did not take to you from the word go.'

'Mrs Roebourne was a disinterested and at times harsh mother, who in my opinion should never have had children in the first place,' she blurted unguardedly.

Mario's dark brows lifted. 'You clashed with her over the handling of the children?' he asked. 'Or perhaps it was because you had designs on her rich husband and wanted her out of the way?'

Sabrina wished she had kept her mouth closed. It seemed no matter what she said she painted herself in a bad light. 'I don't want to talk about it,' she said, picking up her glass again and taking another incautious mouthful.

Mario put his glass down with a dull thud on the table. 'How long did the affair go on?' he asked.

She glared at him resentfully, playing him at his own game. 'What is it to you? You are hardly one to call the pot every shade of black, considering how many affairs you've conducted over the years.'

His dark eyes speared hers. 'I am not denying my sexual profligacy, but to date I have never stolen a married woman from her husband.'

'Marriage is just a piece of paper,' Sabrina threw back. 'It means nothing if the couple are not committed emotionally.'

'So I suppose Howard Roebourne told you his wife was cold and did not understand him?' he said. 'That's the way it usually goes, does it not?'

Sabrina gripped her glass so tightly her fingers went white. 'She was cold and hostile towards her husband, and even the children sometimes. I don't know why he stayed with her, or her with him, to tell you the truth.'

Mario's top lip curled in disgust. 'So you eased his marital suffering by offering your young and nubile body at every available opportunity.'

'Look, Mario,' she said in rapidly rising frustration, 'The Roebournes' marriage was a mess well before I entered the fray. Howard was having an affair—I suspect not his first—with someone else long before I came into their employ.'

Mario studied her for a long moment. Her colour was heightened, her body tense, as if desperate to convince him of her lies. But he wasn't going to fall for it. He'd known Howard for years, and Howard had told him everything—how Sabrina had orchestrated her seduction of him from that very first meeting. She'd had her designs on a potential sugar-daddy, and who better than a wealthy man who was struggling to keep his home life together for the sake of his children? It would take a saint to resist a woman like Sabrina Halliday. She had a sensual allure about her that was intoxicating. That intriguing combination of doe-eyed innocence and surly defiance made every drop of Mario's blood drain from his brain to his groin even now. The way she pouted at him made him want to crush his lips to hers. She could snip and snarl at him all she liked, but it did nothing to disguise the naked hunger he could see in her eyes. Howard Roebourne obviously hadn't been able to satisfy her, which left the field right open for him. And it would be very satisfying, very satisfying indeed, to have her writhing and gasping in his arms.

He could hardly wait.

He topped up her wine glass before attending to his own. 'You expect me to believe your word over his?' he asked.

'What possible reason would I have to lie to you?' she asked, frowning at him.

He leaned back in his chair and surveyed her for another lengthy moment. 'I have no reason to doubt Roebourne's account, having personally experienced your seductive wiles.'

'Oh, for pity's sake!' Sabrina threw back in outrage. 'If anyone is to blame for that kiss, it's you. You took advantage of me.'

His eyes raked her mercilessly. 'Careful, Sabrina,' he warned. 'Those are very serious charges you are laying at my door. Are you sure your recollection of the day in question is accurate?'

Sabrina wasn't sure who she hated more: him for reminding her of her one moment of weakness, or herself for responding to him so feverishly at the time. 'I was not in control of myself,' she said, knowing it sounded rather feeble. 'I don't usually drink more than one glass of alcohol, especially on an empty stomach. If I gave you the wrong impression back then, I am sorry. I can assure you it will not happen again.'

He smiled at her indolently. 'I am counting on it happening again—tomorrow, in fact, when we get married. The groom always gets to kiss the bride, correct?'

Sabrina felt her eyes widen to the size of the soup bowl in front of her. *'Tomorrow?'* she choked.

'I have applied for a special licence,' he said evenly. 'The magistrate has made special dispensation in order for us to travel to Italy as Molly's legal guardians. I have already activated the adoption formalities, but they will take some time.'

Sabrina felt as if her life was spinning out of control. She had comforted herself with the hope that she would at least have a few days to get used to the idea of marrying Mario and moving abroad. Now it seemed she would barely have enough time to pack a bag before she was legally his wife. Her heart began to hammer in panic. It was too soon. She needed more time. But then would *any* amount of time be enough?

'Of course it will by necessity have to be a registry-office affair,' Mario continued.

'Too bad if I wanted a white wedding with all the trimmings,' Sabrina put in, unable to refrain from sounding churlish.

His eyes glinted with derision. 'A white wedding?' he asked. 'Would that not be rather hypocritical, given your sexual history?'

She brought up her chin. 'Most women regardless of their sexual experience dream of being a proper bride,' she said. 'It's the one day in a girl's life she can feel like a princess.'

He sat looking at her for so long without speaking, Sabrina began to wish she hadn't spoken. She sat, trying not to squirm in her chair, her cheeks growing hotter by the second, her stomach in tight knots and her girlhood dreams in tatters. Just like her mother, all she had ever wanted was to be married—to wear a beautiful dress and veil, to wear something old, something new, something borrowed and something blue. But just like her mother she was going to be cheated out of it. She chided herself for being so sentimental. It wasn't as if it was going to be a real marriage in any case. And it was certainly not going to last any length of time if Mario had his way. But still…

'I fail to see why you should desire a huge fuss for a marriage that for all intents and purposes will not be a normal one,' Mario said, voicing her thoughts out loud.

'That's not the point,' she said. 'People with the sort of wealth and public profile you possess will expect you to have a proper wedding, not some hole-in-the-corner affair.'

Mario began to drum his fingers on the table, his eyes still tethering hers. 'What is this about, Sabrina?' he asked.

She caught her bottom lip between her teeth. 'Nothing,' she said. 'Forget I said anything. You're right—a registry office makes perfect sense under the circumstances.'

Mario wondered what she was playing at. Did she hope to make him think twice about ending the marriage by making him commit to the formality of a full-blown, church-sanctified ceremony? He was Italian, after all; the church was a deeply entrenched part of his culture, and she could hardly be ignorant of it. She was a devious little madam, perhaps far more devious than he had first allowed. Did she want the world to know she had landed herself a wealthy business tycoon? Perhaps, to whitewash her reputation over her involvement with Howard Roebourne. But there was no way Mario was going to dance to her particular tune. He would marry her—but on his terms and his terms only.

'I have chartered a private jet for our trip to Rome,' he said, changing the subject. 'I thought it would make it more comfortable for Molly. Long-haul flights are not the most pleasant experience in a commercial plane, even in business class, and particularly so for an infant, I would imagine.'

'You seemed to have thought of everything,' she said, still looking at him with a sulky expression.

'I am doing my best to cover all bases,' he answered. 'However, I have not yet purchased a wedding or engagement ring for you to wear. I thought I would wait until we are in Rome. I have a jeweller friend who acts as an agent for the Marcolini diamonds.'

She gave a 'couldn't care less' shrug. 'You can get one from a fairground slot machine for all I care. I am quite sure that's what you would really prefer to do.'

Mario felt his jaw lock with tension. 'Do not push me too far, Sabrina,' he said. 'It is not too late for me to find someone else to step up to the plate and be a mother to Molly.'

Her grey eyes were stormy as they warred with his. 'I am not going away without a fight,' she said. 'I am going to hate every minute of being married to you, but I love Molly enough to endure whatever torture you dish out.'

Mario tossed his napkin aside, his mouth set in an intractable line. 'You can hate me all you like, but one thing I absolutely insist on is that you keep your ill feelings out of the sight and hearing of Molly. She might be too young to speak as yet, but she has eyes and ears. I do not want her poisoned against me by you.'

Sabrina wished her nails were long enough to score down

his arrogant face. Anger raged inside her, red spots of it almost blinding her as she returned his heated glare. How she hated him! He was everything she most despised in a man. She was unused to feeling such powerful, overwhelming emotions. She was normally such an even-tempered person, slow to anger, patient to a fault—and yet in Mario Marcolini's presence something inside her burned like a hot flame, threatening to totally consume her. But she knew if she gave in to her fury he would use it against her. He had the power to do whatever he wanted. She would never see Molly again, and he would not have a twinge of conscience about it.

In less than twenty-four hours they would be married. That would at least give her some sort of security and a rightful place in Molly's life, for the time being at least. All she could hope for was that he would see in time how much Molly needed her and allow her a permanent place in the little girl's life, even if it meant she had to suffer regular contact with him as joint custodian.

Taking a deep breath to calm herself down, she picked up her wine glass and took another sip, all the time watching the way Mario's dark eyes surveyed her with brooding intensity. 'You know something, Mario?' she said after a moment. 'I think that works both ways, don't you? If Molly hears you calling me names and other such opprobrious names, what sort of husband and father figure will she think you are?'

He reached for his glass, his eyes still on hers. 'I dare say we will both have to watch our tongues when interacting with each other,' he conceded. 'But I am sure all parents have to at times shelve their differences for the sake of their children.'

'Children are highly perceptive,' Sabrina pointed out. 'They can nearly always sense when their parents are at loggerheads, even when the parents think they are hiding it. It can cause great emotional distress for youngsters when they feel undercurrents of tension all the time.'

'Then we will have to make sure we settle our differences well before Molly is of an age to be affected by them,' he returned.

'How do you suggest we do that?' Sabrina asked, frowning in wariness.

'We shall have to call a truce,' he said, raising his glass in preparation for a toast. 'How about we make a toast?'

She cautiously touched her glass against his. 'What exactly are we drinking to?' she asked.

He gave her an enigmatic smile. 'To making love, not war,' he said and, lifting his glass to his lips, he drained the contents.

CHAPTER SIX

SABRINA put her glass down on the table with a hand that trembled slightly. 'I…I need to check on Molly,' she said, and pushed back her chair.

Mario got to his feet. 'I have a few calls to make and some emails to send, but I will do it downstairs in the business centre so I don't disturb Molly,' he said. 'Feel free to get into bed whenever you are ready.'

Sabrina felt her body tense. 'Um…I think I would be more comfortable sleeping on the sofa,' she said.

His eyes smouldered as they held hers. 'You do not fancy sharing my bed, Sabrina?' he asked. 'What—is it too soon after leaving Roebourne's?'

She tightened her mouth, refusing to respond to his taunt, beyond caring if it confirmed his opinion of her as a tart. Let him think what he liked. He was hardly one to throw the first stone, given his easy-come easy-go approach to the women in his life.

Mario came to stand in front of her, blocking her exit. 'I can make you forget all about him,' he said.

Sabrina sucked in a breath when he stroked his fingertip down her cheek to just within reach of her mouth. Every sensitive nerve in her face bloomed in response. Her lips began to tingle; the anticipation of feeling the brush of his mouth against hers became almost unbearable. Her eyes were trapped by the mesmerising heat of his, the silent communication of attraction and hot-blooded desire making her heart begin to pound and her legs feel as if they were turning to water.

She watched as his mouth slowly descended towards hers, millimetre by millimetre, the light, warm breeze of his breath caressing her expectant lips, thrilling them, ramping up her excitement until she was tilting towards him, her eyes fluttering closed as his mouth finally, blissfully met hers.

It was a potently explosive kiss. But then Sabrina wondered if any of Mario's kisses were anything else. Everything about him communicated his sexual power, most particularly his utterly sensual mouth. She felt the hot, hard heat of him as his mouth commandeered hers, his lips firm and demanding, and yet strangely gentle and persuasive. She opened her mouth on a shuddering sigh, her whole body shaking in reaction when his tongue drove through the small opening in a thrust-like movement, an erotic imitation of what his lower body would do if she let her resolve slip.

She felt him explore every corner of her mouth in erotic detail, his teeth taking her bottom lip in a nip-like tug that sent a zigzag of lightning down her spine. His tongue tangled with hers again, playing with it, teasing it, stroking it and then subduing it, reminding her just exactly who was in control. It certainly wasn't her, Sabrina thought ruefully. She was giving a pretty fair imitation of a lustful libertine, and yet there seemed to be nothing she could do to stop it.

As soon as his lips met hers, she felt as if he had turned a

FREE BOOKS OFFER

To get you started, we'll send you
2 FREE books and a FREE gift

There's no catch, everything is **FREE**

Accepting your 2 **FREE** books and **FREE** mystery gift
places you under no obligation to buy anything.

Be part of the Mills & Boon® Book Club™ and receive your favourite
Series books up to 2 months before they are in the shops and delivered
straight to your door. Plus, enjoy a wide range of **EXCLUSIVE** benefits!

- Best new women's fiction – delivered right to
  your door with FREE P&P

- Avoid disappointment – get your books up to
  2 months before they are in the shops

- No contract – no obligation to buy

2 **FREE** books
and a
FREE gift

We hope that after receiving your free books you'll
want to remain a member. But the choice is yours.
So why not give us a go? You'll be glad you did!

Visit **millsandboon.co.uk** to stay up to date
with offers and to sign-up for our newsletter

P9HI9

Mrs/Miss/Ms/Mr	Initials

BLOCK CAPITALS PLEASE

Surname

Address

Postcode

Email

☺™ MILLS & BOON®
Pure reading pleasure

The Mills & Boon® Book Club™ – Here's how it works:

Accepting your free books places you under no obligation to buy anything. You may keep the books and gift and return the despatch note marked "cancel". If we do not hear from you, about a month later we'll send you 4 brand new books and invoice you £3.19*each. That is the complete price – there is no extra charge for post and packaging. You may cancel at any time, otherwise we will send you 4 stories a month which you may purchase or return to us – the choice is yours.

*Terms and prices subject to change without notice.

NO STAMP NEEDED!

MILLS & BOON®
Book Club

FREE BOOK OFFER
FREEPOST NAT 10298
RICHMOND
TW9 1BR

NO STAMP
NECESSARY
IF POSTED IN
THE U.K. OR N.I.

switch on in her body. It was programmed to respond to him and only him. It wasn't that she hadn't been kissed before, but never so thoroughly, and never to the point where her body melted like honey under a blow torch. She could feel the slick moisture of desire between her thighs, her intimate cleft swelling with need, the on-off pulse deep inside her aching for the delicious friction of his thick, hard possession. She could feel him against her, the outline of his maleness inciting her to kiss him back with heated fervour. Her tongue was stroking his boldly, her teeth tugging at his lips, both top and bottom, in little kittenish bites that brought a primitive groan of approval from deep within him.

'*Lei è una tentatrice,*' he growled, and deepened the kiss even further, pushing her back against the wall, his hands going to the proud mounds of her breasts.

Sabrina felt her spine almost collapse when he cupped her, for even through the layers of her clothing she felt the exhilarating electricity of his touch. But, impatient to feel her skin on skin, he tugged her top out of her skirt, and with a deftness that spoke of his monumental experience he unclipped her bra, freeing her aching, swollen breasts to the ministrations of his warm, caressing hands.

It was mind-blowing to feel her nipples embed themselves in his warm palms, the intimacy of his touch taking her by surprise, and yet delighting her at the same time. The weight and shape of her breasts seemed to be a perfect match for the cup of his hands. Never had she felt so feminine, so in tune with her body. Every pore of her skin seemed to be throbbing with feeling, her senses shuddering with the need for fulfilment. She squirmed against him, rubbing against his touch, wanting more, so much more.

She wanted to feel his hot mouth sucking on her, to feel those white, hard teeth of his pulling on her erect nipples, to feel the rasp of his tongue on her sensitive flesh, to feel him delight in her femaleness as she was delighting in everything that made him a man: the evening shadow peppering his jaw, the insistent pressure of his mouth, the driving heat of his tongue, and the thundering pulse of his blood that left her in no doubt of his erection and the pressure for release building within him. She could feel his hardness against her, so tantalisingly close to where her body ached and pulsed with need.

Her mind began to picture him, imagining how long and thick he was. She was shocked at where her thoughts were leading her, but with his magical mouth setting hers alight and his hands shaping her so possessively she was lost to the traitorous workings of her brain.

His mouth moved from its sensual assault of hers to suckle her right breast, the moistness, the heat and fire of him making her gasp out loud. The caress of his hands on the creamy, smooth skin of her breasts had sent her pulses soaring, but the feel of his tongue rolling over her tightly budded nipple was beyond anything she had felt before. Her nerves exploded with feeling as the rasp of his tongue circled her before he drew on her with his hot, moist mouth.

Desire flooded her being, sending sparks up and down her spine, buckling her legs, loosening every ligament, until she felt as if she was going to melt into a pool at his feet. She dug her fingers into the thick thatch of his hair, holding on to anchor herself as he subjected her to even more of his earth-shattering caresses. Every nerve-ending fizzed with sensation. She was on fire for him, every atom of her being screaming for the fulfilment he was holding, tantalisingly just out of her reach.

Just when she thought she could take no more, his mouth came back to hers, swallowing her whimper of pleasure as his tongue found hers and swept it up in a dance that shook her to the core of her being. She clung to him, her body pressed so tightly against him she felt every hard ridge of him, each point of contact thrilling her beyond description. Her mind took her on another erotic journey, conjuring up images of his body naked against hers, their limbs entwined, their bodies rocking in the quest for satiation.

Almost without realising she was doing it, Sabrina slid her hands down his back, exploring the well-formed, tightly bunched muscles that even his shirt could not disguise. She went lower, underneath his jacket, to feel the tautness of his buttocks, her stomach giving a little hollow gulp when she felt him surge against her in response to her touch.

The need to feel him in her hands, to shape the hot, hard potency of his aroused body, was a temptation she suddenly could not resist. With tentative shyness her hands skimmed over his slim hips before she brushed against the front of his trousers where the fabric was stretched with the heated trajectory of his arousal. She stroked his outline, her fingertips quivering at the latent power of him. She felt him flinch, as if her touch had burned him, and a rough, primal-sounding groan sounded from deep within his throat as his mouth ground against hers with increasing fervour.

Suddenly the kiss was over.

Mario stepped back, capturing both of her shameless hands in one of his, a blade of disdain sharpening his dark-as-pitch gaze. 'You know, that is quite some sensual repertoire you have perfected, Sabrina,' he said. 'I was within moments of letting you have your wicked way with me.'

Sabrina had to give herself a mental shake to reorient herself. Her senses were skyrocketing all over the place, her heart-rate galloping, her lips still throbbing and her colour at an all-time high. She lowered her gaze and, wrenching out of his hold quickly, covered herself, hating him for making her lose control in such an abandoned way. No doubt he had done it deliberately, showing how he could pick her up and put her down like a toy that amused him one minute and bored him the next.

When she finally met his gaze once more, she made sure her features were blank, even though her body was still screaming out in frustration. 'It was just a kiss, Mario,' she said in an offhand tone. 'It was never going to be anything more than that.'

'Perhaps. But if you change your mind about occupying that sofa, let me know,' he said with a glinting smile. 'You never know where the next kiss might lead, now, do you?'

It annoyed Sabrina that he was so clearly unaffected by what had happened just moments earlier. He showed no signs of a man pushed to the limits of physical control. Instead he looked cool and calm as if they had done nothing more than exchange a quick, platonic peck on the cheek.

She on the other hand felt completely undone; her emotions were all over the place, not one of them making any sense to her. She wasn't in love with him, far from it, but neither was she as immune to him as she so dearly wanted to be. What was it about him that made her feel so out of sorts?

Well, maybe that wasn't so hard to answer after all. He had 'casual sex' written all over him. She had known it the moment Laura had introduced her to him the day of her wedding. The memory was as clear as if it had been yesterday.

'Just wait until you meet Ric's best man, Mario Marcolini,' Laura had said with a twinkling smile as she'd made a last-minute adjustment to her veil. 'I am sure you two will get on like a house on fire.'

Sabrina had rolled her eyes as she'd handed Laura another bobby pin. 'I hope you are not trying to match make, Laura,' she cautioned. 'You know how I feel about that sort of thing.'

Laura had given her a guileless look as she'd slid the pin in place. 'I wouldn't dream of doing any such thing. It's just that Mario is quite a catch. He's disgustingly rich, and now that he's past thirty he's surely going to be thinking about hanging up his playboy hat for something a little more substantial in terms of a relationship. You are perfect for him. It's that "opposites attract" thing. He's a man of the world; you are a young woman who hasn't even been around the corner, let alone the block several times. He's so cynical; you're so fresh and trusting. I tell you, it's a match made in heaven.'

Sabrina had grimaced in embarrassment. 'Oh, please, you don't have to keep reminding me how unsophisticated and in-experienced I am.'

Laura had given her a fond smile. 'Don't be so hard on yourself. Not every man these days wants an experienced temptress in the bedroom. Ric loved the fact he was my first lover. I am so glad I waited. I know it's considered terribly old-fashioned, but I never felt I was ready before I met him. He told me it was the greatest gift I could have given him.'

Sabrina blinked herself back to the present. Mario was looking at her in that cynical way of his, probably thinking of how he could cajole her into his bed with the crook of one finger. 'If you want a wife in the real sense of the word, you are going to have to pay for it,' she said, goaded beyond reasonable caution.

He gave her a mocking look as he reached inside his jacket for his wallet. He unfolded it, took out a thick wad of notes and fanned them out on the coffee table next to her like a hand of cards. 'I hope that covers the entertainment so far,' he said. 'It was quite a floor show. I am looking forward to an encore.'

Sabrina glowered at him, her anger towards him like a swirling hot tide of lava inside her. 'You think you can get whatever you want by opening your wallet, don't you?'

His hard gaze raked her mercilessly. 'I know I can, Sabrina,' he drawled. 'You, my little gold-digger, just proved it.'

Sabrina thought of several stinging retorts to hurl his way, but before she could utter even one of them he had turned on his heel and left.

The sofa in the end made quite a comfortable bed, and even though Sabrina hadn't expected to be able to relax enough to sleep she found herself drifting off regardless. Molly was asleep in her pram nearby, and apart from the occasional snuffle she slept soundly until about four in the morning, when she began to whimper on and off.

When it was clear Molly wasn't going to settle back down again, Sabrina turned on a lamp and changed the baby's nappy before heating her bottle. Once Molly was fed, Sabrina sat on the sofa and gently rocked the pram with her foot to settle the baby back to sleep.

The front door opened and Mario came in, still dressed in the clothes he had been wearing earlier, although he'd pulled his shirt free from the waistband of his trousers. His hair looked as if he had run his fingers through it several times, and his jaw was heavily shadowed with stubble. Although his eyes had shadows beneath, they still contained a devilish light when they collided with hers.

'Waiting up for me, sweet Sabrina?' he asked.

She gave her eyes a quick roll of disdain. 'I can see why you have booked the largest suite in the hotel—no doubt it is to make room for your ego.'

Mario laughed as he undid a couple of buttons on his shirt. 'And I can see how it might be rather fun being married to you. The challenge of taming that quick tongue of yours could prove to be very entertaining.'

Sabrina threw him a filthy look. 'I can't stand men who think they can control the women in their lives.'

'Ah, but you are not really the woman in my life, are you, Sabrina?' he said. 'But perhaps you would like to be, *sì*? That would be the icing on the cake, would it not? A rich man for a husband, a child thrown into the bargain and a lifestyle other people only dream about.'

She gave him a withering look. 'I can think of nothing worse than being tied to you.'

A light of challenge came into his eyes. 'I think you are playing a very clever game,' he said. 'No doubt you have played it many times before. But with me, young lady, you have taken on much more than you realise. I am not going to be manipulated by you. I know what you want and how far you will go to get it. The next thing, you will be telling me you are in love with me and want our marriage to continue indefinitely.'

She rolled her eyes. 'As if.'

Mario smiled. He liked nothing better than a woman who was quick with a come back; it showed a level of intelligence that was a match to his. Sabrina's feisty nature was becoming increasingly attractive to him. He was so used to women simpering around him, bowing to his demands without a whimper of protest.

Sabrina on the other hand fought him tooth and nail, snarling at him like a cat cornered by a snapping terrier. It made him all the more determined to tame her, to have her purring in submission in his arms, welcoming him like a lioness who recognised the alpha male of the pride, giving herself to him because she realised there was no other male who could satisfy her the way he could.

And he *could* satisfy her. He knew it as surely as he knew where his next breath was coming from. He had not felt anything like the heat he felt in her kiss; he had not felt anything like the fire in her touch as her hands had skimmed over him, barely touching, but setting fires on his flesh all the same. His skin was still smouldering, the ashes of banked down desire still glowing, threatening to erupt into consuming flames if she so much as pressed her soft mouth to his.

'I am going to catch a couple of hours' sleep,' Mario said. 'Are you sure you will not join me in my bed?'

The disparaging look she gave him made his skin tighten all over with excitement.

Later today she would be his wife.

Legally.

Officially.

And from what he had seen and tasted of her so far he did not think it would be too long before she agreed to be his wife in every sense of the word.

CHAPTER SEVEN

THE registry-office ceremony was just as disappointing as Sabrina had imagined it would be. A disinterested official conducted the short, impersonal exchange of vows and the paperwork was signed and sealed in less time than it would have taken a real bride to walk down the aisle of a church. The only thing that stood out for Sabrina was the part where the marriage celebrant gave Mario permission to kiss the bride.

Sabrina had been preparing herself for that moment for hours, but even so when his mouth came down on hers she felt every bone in her body melt. Her lips clung to his, her body sinking into the leanly muscled strength of his tall frame. The kiss was brief but intense—but because Mario was the first to bring an end to it Sabrina felt cheated, wondering if he knew she was secretly longing for more. It was so hard to read his expression; he gave no indication of the event of their marriage affecting him whatsoever, which in a perverse sort of way upset her even more.

The press were in their droves on the street outside, but Mario had already organised a security team to keep them at bay. It was impossible to prevent them from taking a few snapshots, however, and Sabrina was glad she had gone to the trouble of wearing her best outfit, a pale-pink suit and a string of pearls and earrings that had belonged to her mother. She had piled her hair in a casual but still elegant knot on her head, and taken extra care with her make-up, recognising she was now playing a role that required all the poise and sophistication she could muster. She didn't want any of Mario's previous and future lovers to look at her and think he had married trailer trash. She was determined to show everyone, including Mario himself, that she was a young woman who knew how to carry herself in the public eye.

There was no reception following the service, no crystal flutes of the best champagne to toast the future, no throwing of the bouquet—there wasn't even a single flower for her to toss. Instead there was a flurry of activity as Mario's driver ushered them into the waiting limousine to take them to the airport for her departure to Rome.

Molly thankfully had slept through the proceedings and didn't wake until Sabrina had to lift her out of her baby carrier in order to go through the security check-point.

In no time at all they were led to the waiting jet, and once the safety demonstration was over, the sleek plane taxied along the runway before it finally took off like a giant metallic bird.

Sabrina was glad she had Molly's needs and comfort to see to as it kept her attention away from the silent figure seated beside her. She was intensely aware of him, however. He only had to turn over the page of the thick folder of documents he was reading for her to shiver in reaction at the occasional brush of his arm against hers.

Eventually the stress and emotional turmoil of the day got the better of her, and, with Molly asleep in the bassinet against the bulkhead, Sabrina closed her eyes, promising herself she would have a little power-nap to refresh herself before Molly next woke.

Mario breathed in the sweet light fragrance of Sabrina's light brown hair as she leant against his shoulder. She smelt of fresh spring flowers, sweet peas and jasmine, a subtle but alluring combination that made his concentration drift away from the article on fund management he was supposed to be reading.

He looked at her small, slim hands lying on his right thigh, their ringless state reminding him of his need to organise an engagement and wedding ring to add credence to their sudden marriage.

He had phoned his brother and briefly explained the situation, and Antonio had encouraged him to concentrate on what was best for Molly. Building a long-term relationship with Sabrina was not something Mario had ever considered, but he was starting to see how the baby responded to Sabrina as if she was indeed her biological mother. He didn't want to think too far into the future, but he comforted himself that lots of children survived the divorce of their parents or guardians. Being stuck in a loveless marriage was not an option for him; his parents had enjoyed a mostly happy and fulfilling relationship up until his father had suffered a fatal heart attack. His mother's decline over the last five years and recent death had made Mario even more convinced marriage was not for him. He didn't like the thought of being dependent on someone for anything, including emotional support. He had seen what had happened to Antonio and his wife, how the tragedy of their stillborn first child had torn them apart for five long years.

Did he want that sort of emotion in his life? It was hard

enough being responsible for Molly, whom he loved as if she was indeed his own. He didn't like the uncertainty, the sense of vulnerability, that giving all of yourself to another person created. He had never been in love, and often wondered if it was an overrated emotion to cover more base desires, which in the end usually burned out all by themselves. He knew too many married couples who could barely stand the sight of each other, grudgingly staying together for the sake of children or combined assets.

Even if he had been thinking along the lines of marriage Sabrina was not the sort of woman Mario had ever envisaged as wife material. She might have a knack with infants and children, but what man wanted a wife who was likely to stray at the first opportunity? For the duration of their marriage he would have to keep a very close eye on her. He didn't want her making a fool of him behind his back. He was the first to admit he had more than his share of pride, and he had no doubt from what he had seen so far that Sabrina was just the type who would find it entertaining to grind it into the dust.

Although, looking at her now totally relaxed in sleep, it was hard to imagine her with the bed-hopping reputation she had been tarred with. He supposed that was why she was so successful at luring unsuspecting men into her orbit. She had a little-girl-lost look at times that had the potential to confound the hardest of hearts. He knew he had to watch himself around her. He was so used to playing the game with women who had the same motives as himself: sex without ties, fun on the run, nothing permanent and certainly no emotional investment. Sabrina challenged all that with one look with those smoky-grey eyes, not to mention her all-female body with its promise of passion in every delicious curve.

Mario moved his arm to encircle her as she nestled closer. A soft sigh escaped her lips, her hands moving farther up his thigh to where his blood was already pumping like a piston. She was so practised at her game she could seduce a man in her sleep, he thought wryly.

She murmured something and lifted her head, blinking at him groggily. 'What time is it?' she asked, brushing at her disordered hair, the action releasing another whiff of its fragrance into the air.

'Rome time or Sydney time?' he asked, trying to resist the urge to tuck a loose tendril of her hair behind her ear.

She straightened in her seat, her eyes going straight to the sleeping baby. 'Has she woken?'

'No, she slept like a…' He suddenly smiled. 'Like a baby.'

Sabrina turned and looked at him, her heart giving a little jerky movement in her chest at his smile. The smile had travelled all the way up to his eyes, making him look so utterly gorgeous that her breath stalled. She swallowed and tore her gaze away, concentrating with fierce intent on the sleeping baby. 'Yes, well, whoever made up that adage obviously hadn't had a baby,' she said to fill the silence.

'Perhaps you are right,' he said, stretching out his legs.

'How soon before we land?' she asked as she looked out of the window to distract herself from the proximity of his long legs so close to hers.

'The pilot has already started his descent,' he said. 'It won't be long before the cabin crew will want us to prepare for landing. It seems a shame to wake Molly, but she is safer strapped in one of our laps than in the cot.'

The announcement came through as Mario had predicted, and Sabrina cuddled Molly close as he helped fix the infant seatbelt-attachment to hers. She barely breathed as his long-fingered hands dealt with the clip and straps, her stomach sucked in tightly in case he inadvertently or indeed deliberately touched her. She could feel her heart doing crazy backflips at his proximity, the masculine scent of him dancing around her face.

Before he sat back in his seat his gaze found hers, holding it for a pulsing beat or two of silence. Sabrina was the first to pull her gaze away, her desperate attempt to act cool and composed spoilt somewhat by the blush she could feel spreading over her cheeks. She drew Molly close and, taking a shallow breath, settled back in her seat as the plane began to make its way down.

Within a few minutes they were safely on the ground and soon after they'd made their way through customs, and finally to the chauffeur-driven vehicle waiting outside. The press took a couple of photographs, and Sabrina noticed Mario seemed to be particularly annoyed by the intrusion as he swore at one of the paparazzi as he shouldered his way past, keeping Molly close against his chest.

Sabrina absorbed the view as they drove towards the city. The ancient ruins of the Colosseum went past, and a flicker of excitement travelled through her belly in spite of the circumstances of their paper marriage. Her only overseas trip prior to this had been to New Zealand, and, although stunningly beautiful and with its own ancient Maori history, it was nothing like the eternal city of Rome. There was so much to see, so much history and so much beauty, it was almost too much for her to take in.

Mario pointed out the various points of interest along the way, including the Celian Hill and then the Vatican in the distance. 'I will be busy at work but I will organise someone to accompany you on a guided tour of all the sights,' he offered as they drew close to his *palazzo*.

Sabrina was surprised at the tiny jab of disappointment she felt. It wasn't as if she even liked his company; why then should she want him to be the one to show her around? 'I am sure I will be perfectly able to find my way around by myself,' she said as the car purred to a stop outside an imposing-looking *palazzo*.

'I am sure you are more than capable, but I must insist on Molly's welfare being attended to at all times,' he said as he helped her out of the car. 'Rome is a beautiful city, but like a lot of cities its size it has it dangers—congested traffic being one of them. You are not used to cars being on the other side of the road, for instance. You would only have to push Molly's pram out on the road ahead of you for tragedy to strike if you were not concentrating.'

Sabrina could see his point, but she couldn't help noticing it was Molly's safety he was primarily concerned about, not hers. If anything it could prove to be rather convenient for him if something was to happen to her. He hadn't wanted a wife, and certainly not one with the sort of reputation she had.

She pushed her pique aside as Mario led the way inside the *palazzo*. The housekeeper came bustling towards them, barely gracing Sabrina with a glance before turning in delight at the baby, who was soundly asleep in the baby carrier.

Mario made a few cursory introductions, but it was clear to Sabrina he had been brutally honest with his staff about the woman he had married. A hard nut of anger lodged in her throat and she clenched her teeth behind her coolly polite smile each time another staff member was introduced to her. She was determined to have it out with Mario in private, however. Surely it had been unnecessary to swing the jury before she had even stepped over the threshold?

It didn't help that everyone spoke Italian in a rapid-fire manner that made it impossible for her to pick up some of the very few words she had managed to learn from Laura. It made her feel all the more shut out, as if they were determined not to make any allowances for her.

'Giovanna will show you to your room,' Mario informed her. 'I have to call in at my office to catch up on some paperwork which needs my immediate attention. I will no doubt see you later this evening.'

Sabrina wondered if the paperwork he was going to catch up on was slim and blonde with breasts you could serve a meal off. She pushed her resentment down with an effort, turned and followed the housekeeper up the huge flight of stairs, trying not to show how overawed she was by the opulent furnishings on the way. Priceless works of art hung upon the walls, marble statues and busts were displayed along the lower and upper landings, and even the runner of carpet that followed the curve of the staircase felt as it if had been woven from air.

The housekeeper opened a door about halfway down the second-floor landing. 'This your room,' she said. 'The *bambino* next door. Signore Marcolini next door to that.'

Sabrina thanked her, and without another word Giovanna left with a disapproving rustle of her starched, black uniform.

Molly made a noise from the carrier, and Sabrina sighed and bent down to take her out. She held her close, silently promising she would see this through for the baby's sake, no matter how difficult it turned out to be.

Sabrina resisted falling asleep too early in case she couldn't sleep that night. She felt jet-lagged, but with Molly to bathe and feed it gave her a focus to keep going. But once Molly was settled in the nursery next to her room there was little else for her to do but wait until it was a reasonable time to go to bed.

The housekeeper had informed her earlier that evening that dinner would be served at eight-thirty, but when Sabrina went downstairs she ended up eating alone as Mario hadn't yet returned. There was no message from him that she could find, and although she longed to ask Giovanna if Mario had told her when he would be back she resisted doing so.

The large dining-room with its solitary place-setting on the highly polished, seemingly endless table made her feel all the more isolated. The food was delicious, however, and although her appetite was affected by the change of time zone she still managed to do the meal justice. She even drank a glass of wine, figuring it would help her to relax when it came time to go to bed.

She thought about waiting until Mario got home to speak to him about the housekeeper's coldness towards her, especially in view of Molly—who although still so young would before too long become aware of undercurrents of tension—but she decided against speaking with him until she was more rested. He was hard enough to resist with all her faculties working; God only knew what would happen if she locked horns with him in the edgy state she was currently in. She felt jittery and agitated, restless and frustrated. Trapped might be a better word, Sabrina thought as she finished the last of her wine. She was trapped by her own traitorous thoughts of Mario pleasuring her, introducing her to the sensual world of sexual pleasure. She felt a little shudder rumble through her as she remembered the passion in his kiss, the teasing of his tongue and the way her body had responded.

Was this energy always going to be simmering between them? she wondered. Or was he dealing with his desire by taking the edge off it with his mistress? Jealousy tightened Sabrina's insides to coils of barbed wire. She hated thinking about him with another woman—*any* other woman. For all the weeks since that kiss she had tortured herself with thoughts of his mouth passionately exploring other women's mouths. It was stupid of her to act like a put-upon wife, but she couldn't help it. She had taken his name and she was damned if she was going to be made of fool of, even if it was just in front of his household staff.

Sabrina made her way upstairs and, once she was confident Molly was still sleeping peacefully, she found herself eyeing the other door leading off the nursery. What would it hurt to have a quick peek into Mario's domain? He wasn't home, and even if he did return she would surely hear him come along the landing, as she had heard Giovanna earlier. She wavered for a moment. *Will I or won't I?* The temptation was dangling there, just waiting for her to give in to it.

There was so much she didn't know about her new husband. Surely it was her right to inspect his private quarters? How else could she find out who he was, what he liked, what he didn't like, what things he chose to have around his private space? She had read somewhere that the three keys to knowing someone was to meet their family, go for a drive with them behind the wheel, and look into their bedroom. Well, Sabrina hadn't yet met Mario's older brother, but she had been for a drive with Mario behind the wheel, so this was the next step. Maybe she was rationalising her intrusion into his privacy, but he had railroaded her into marriage, so surely she had a right to get her own back?

Sabrina watched as her hand slowly reached out to the door knob. It was still not too late to pull back, but instead of doing so she turned it clockwise and the door opened. And then, taking an uneven breath, she stepped over the threshold.

It was a very masculine room.

A large, king-size bed was made up with linen that looked every bit as luxurious as that on her own bed two doors away, but instead of the pink-and-white ensemble on her bed his was starkly black and white. The bedside tables followed the theme; they were black marble, and the lamp-stands polished white marble, the shades a muted grey.

Sabrina could smell him in the air she breathed, the hint of his aftershave, the musk of his male body, and something else she felt drawn to in a way she could neither explain nor understand.

She wandered over to the huge bed, stroking her hand over the spread, her fingertips tingling with sensation as she thought about his long, strong body stretched out in sleep or in the process of hot, passionate sex. How many women had he entertained in here? How many women had he pleasured with his leanly toned body—not to mention that sensual mouth of his?

Sabrina stumbled backwards from her wayward thoughts, only to come up against a wall of warm, hard, male muscle. She spun round, her eyes going wide when she came face to face with Mario. 'I…I was just…just…' Her voice trailed off, her colour rising, her heart stuttering behind her ribcage like a two-stroke engine.

Mario's cynical gaze stripped her naked. 'Come to play, Sabrina?' he asked.

Sabrina brushed at her loose hair with a hand that wasn't quite steady. 'I was just, um, looking around.' It sounded so pathetic, so contrived. It sounded like a woman who was on the prowl, and she could see from the dark glint in his eyes that was exactly the way he had read it.

'Looking around for what?' he said, snaking an arm out to block her exit, his eyes like steel darts pinning hers.

She felt the searing brand of his hand on her forearm, his long fingers overlapping each other around her slim wrist. The air pulsed with tension, a tension she could feel passing from his body to hers. It was as if by merely touching their blood was heating, the temperature rising by the second, until she felt sure she was going to boil unless he let her go. 'N-nothing,' she said in a cracked whisper.

He pulled her up close to his body, chest to chest, thigh to thigh, temptation to temptation. 'We both know what you are looking for, don't we, Sabrina?'

Sabrina could see her own desire reflected in the black pits of his eyes. His pupils were dilated, so much so she had trouble distinguishing the irises from them. Could he see what she was feeling? she wondered. Could he see how she longed for his mouth to capture hers and titillate her senses into overload?

The tip of her tongue came out over her lips, and her stomach folded as his eyes dipped to follow its movement. His eyes came back to hers, the message in them plucking at the strings of her desire, playing a melody she had no hope of resisting. She felt each and every one of the vibrations throughout her body, her breasts aching as they pushed against the lacy restraint of her bra. Her legs felt unsteady, her heart rate equally so. Her body was suddenly outside of her control; it was acting of its own accord, doing things she had not thought possible just a few moments ago. It was moving against his, seeking his hot, hard heat, her hips melting into the thrust and grind of his like the wanton woman he took her to be.

'God damn you,' he growled and, bringing his head down, crushed her mouth beneath his.

It was just like his last two kisses, explosive and out of control within seconds. Sabrina relished every sweep and thrust of his brandy-scented tongue; she revelled in every guttural groan he tried to suppress as she moved against him instinctively. It felt so good to be in his embrace; it felt so right for some strange reason. Her body fitted so neatly against his, her feminine softness against his hardness in a way that made her feel as if this was meant to be, that this moment was inevitable, and had been from the moment they had first met. That first spark of interest in his dark eyes had awakened her femininity, made her become aware of her body and its needs, and how only he could meet them. No one else had affected her the way he did. She didn't think anyone else could, not now she had been singed by the sensual heat of his touch.

She could have stopped him, she *should* have stopped him, but still she returned his kiss—inciting him to caress her breasts, to shape them with his hands, to tug her clothes out of the way so he could feel her skin on skin, so he could open his mouth over one erect nipple, sucking, licking and drawing on her until she was whimpering in pleasure. He moved to her other breast, subjecting it to the same passionate assault before he pressed her backwards towards the bed.

Sabrina considered telling him of her inexperience. She even opened her mouth in that brief moment when his left hers, but all she could manage to say was his name: 'Mario…'

His dark eyes swept over her hungrily, making her blood race through her veins at a terrifying pace. 'I told myself I would not do this,' he said, breathing hard. 'But the truth is I have wanted to do this since the first day we met.'

'I wanted it too,' she breathed against his lips as they sealed hers again with a kiss that left her in no doubt of where they were heading from here.

Sabrina felt the mattress at the back of her knees, but even then she didn't stop him. It was like someone else was in charge of her senses; it wasn't the sensible Sabrina Halliday who rarely dated, let alone kissed a man she barely knew. It was someone else, a sensual addict who pulsed and throbbed with lust for a man she all but hated.

She fell back on the bed with his weight coming over her, his muscled thighs entrapping hers, his hands dealing with her clothes in much the same manner as she was dealing with his—frantically. Buttons popped, fabric ripped, and still it didn't register that she should call a halt. She wanted this. She wanted to feel his passion, she wanted to feel him lose control because of her, because of the electric heat that had been passing between them like lightning bolts from the moment they had met.

She lay beneath him, naked except for her knickers, her body writhing beneath the one last barrier that separated them. He had somehow dispensed with everything but his briefs, his aroused length pushing against that final, fragile shield like a tightly clenched fist pushing its way against a pair of closed velvet curtains.

She sucked in a breath as he drew the lace from her body, the slow but steady slide of fabric down her thighs making her arch her spine in readiness for him. She quickly moistened her mouth. 'Mario...' she began. 'I'm not—' She stopped, pulled up short by the fear of him not going on if she told him the truth. She wanted this so much; she needed him to make her feel complete. Stopping now would leave them both stranded and unsatisfied.

His eyes questioned hers. 'Sabrina?'

She ran her hands over his broad shoulders, relishing in the feel of the strength in his bunched muscles. Somehow she wasn't so sure about hating him as much now. She wasn't quite sure if it was possible to hate someone who had such an amazing ability to make her feel the way she was feeling.

'Nothing,' she said, letting out a breath that prickled like a tiny free-floating thorn in her chest.

After a moment he reached across her to open the bedside-table drawer to retrieve a condom. 'Don't worry,' he said. 'I have protection. We don't want any accidents.'

It was a timely reminder of how many times he had done this in the past, but somehow Sabrina managed to ignore that in order to follow the instincts of her body. She watched as he sheathed himself, his length sending another wave of feverish excitement through her.

He positioned her beneath him, locking his mouth on hers as he drove into her warm, moist heat in one deep, slick thrust that brought a gasp of sharp pain from Sabrina's mouth into his.

She felt his whole body freeze above hers.

She blinked back the tears that had sprung to her eyes,

feeling exposed in a way that was deeply unsettling as his frowning gaze sought hers.

'What's the matter?' he asked in a gravel-rough tone.

Sabrina chewed at her lip, her eyes falling away from his. 'I…I should have told you.'

He anchored her chin to bring her gaze back to his. 'Should have told me what?' His eyes, those dark, melted-chocolate eyes, contained a flicker of uncertainty, something she had never seen in them before.

She ran the point of her tongue across her lips, the taste of him still lingering there. His body was still encased in hers, hot, hard and stinging her slightly, although she did her best to conceal it. She felt foolish, gauche and foolish, like an immature child pretending to be an adult. She also felt a failure, a miserable failure at pleasuring a man. This was her first sexual experience and it was forever going to linger in her memory as a fiasco of monumental proportions. Shame coursed through her. She felt it in her cheeks, a burning fire that his dark intense gaze was stoking as each throbbing second passed.

'Sabrina?' he prompted.

She fought against the wobble in her voice. 'I—I'm not very experienced.'

Mario slowly eased himself away from her. He had not for a moment considered she was a virgin. How could he have? He thought back over each and every conversation they had had and couldn't remember a single clue to suggest she was anything but the slut the press had made her out to be. If anything she had on one or two occasions actively encouraged him to believe the stories about her were true.

Guilt drove a dagger into his gut, ripping him wide open with remorse. He had hurt her; he had stolen from her the preciousness of her innocence, slaking his lust with no thought for anything but doing it, and doing it roughly and quickly.

For all the years he had been dating and sleeping with partners, he had not once encountered a virgin. All the women he slept with had been as experienced as him, and, in his early-adult years, some even more so.

He was deeply ashamed. He was not used to feeling so out of his depth. He was used to being in control, used to having things his way. He had always trusted his judgement. He had rarely got it wrong in the past.

And yet he had got it horribly wrong about Sabrina.

Horribly, horribly wrong.

He looked at her grey eyes shining with moisture, and another blade of blame sliced through him. He cleared his tight throat, swallowing against the golf ball of guilt that had lodged there.

'Sabrina…' He sat upright, pulling the covers to shield her nakedness, wincing again when he saw her blood on the stark white of the sheet between her slender legs.

'It's all right,' she said, blushing like a rose. 'It was my fault for not telling you. I was going to, but I felt so embarrassed. I let you believe—'

Mario cut the air with a sharp, coarse oath. 'I will not have you take the blame for what just happened,' he insisted. He clawed his fingers through his hair as he got off the bed, turning his back to dispose of the condom, before he reached for a robe.

Once he was covered, he turned back to face her. 'Damn it, Sabrina, I hurt you. I was so rough with you I could have damaged you.' He swallowed again, but his guilt would not move, either up or down; it remained to choke him until he could barely speak. How could she ever be the same after what he had done? He rubbed at the back of his neck, his guilt crawling beneath every pore of his skin. He had acted like an animal. He had hunted her down and mated with her, not taking the time to get to know her as she deserved to be known.

He dragged his gaze back to her slim body lying in his bed. She hardly took up any room, her light weight barely making an impression on the mattress. He was six-feet-four and, although lean, he was close to twice her weight. He couldn't bear to think of how tiny she was. He was disgusted with himself. He could barely stand to be in the same room as her for the shame he felt.

He strode, agitated, to the *en suite*, came back with a warm, damp face cloth and handed it to her. 'Is there anything I can get you?' he asked, deeply ashamed of how inadequate it sounded.

She shook her head, her small fingers clutching at the face cloth, her cheeks going a deeper shade of pink. 'No, thank you. I just need to have a shower and…and get some sleep. I think it was the jet lag, you know? Why I allowed things to get so out of control…'

Mario swore again. 'Do not let me off the hook so lightly, Sabrina. I deserve to be horse-whipped for what I have done.'

Her small, white teeth sank into her bottom lip again, her eyes moving out of reach of his. 'I was with you all the way,' she said so softly he almost didn't hear it.

'Not quite all the way,' he said, and with a ragged sigh left her to dress in privacy.

CHAPTER EIGHT

SABRINA crawled out of Mario's bed and, using the sheet as a wrap, bent down to pick up her scattered clothes. She winced as her inner muscles protested and another wave of embarrassment washed over her.

Stupid. Stupid. Stupid.

What had she been thinking?

She could blame it on the jet lag or the glass of wine she'd had with dinner, but deep down she wondered if that was just a cop out. She knew exactly why she had allowed him to make love to her: she wanted him. It was as simple as that.

Was that wrong?

No, of course not. What young woman of her age worried about having sex with someone they were deeply attracted to? She was old-fashioned, out of date and naïve to think sex was only for those who were in love. She wasn't in love with Mario. She didn't even like him. And yet there was something about him that drew her inexorably towards him. She felt like a small fluttering moth attracted to a dangerously hot flame. She had just got burnt and had only herself to blame.

Sabrina checked on Molly before she went to the *en suite* off her room. After a shower she curled up on her bed, hugging a pillow to her chest, torturing herself with wondering if Mario had left the *palazzo* to have his needs met elsewhere. Her mind began to picture him with his blonde mistress, the catwalk model she had seen him with in the newspapers several times. No doubt *she* would not have flinched at his touch, nor would she have blushed like a schoolgirl at seeing his naked body in full arousal. Sabrina groaned and put the pillow over her face, trying to block the taunting images.

When there was a soft knock at her door, she blinked in surprise. 'Y-yes?' she said.

'Sabrina, it's me,' Mario said. 'May I come in?'

'Um, yes.' She sat upright as he came into the room.

He too had showered. He was dressed in jeans and a T-shirt, not nightwear as she was, but then she assumed he didn't own any. She couldn't imagine that long, leanly muscled body encased in boring old-fashioned flannelette or cotton pyjamas.

His gaze ran over her for a moment. 'How are you feeling?' he asked.

Sabrina felt her face heating under his scrutiny. 'I'm fine.'

He came over to the bed and sat on the edge of the mattress, his brow heavily furrowed. 'Why did you not defend yourself about the Roebourne affair?' he asked.

She hugged her knees to her chest, her flesh tingling with awareness with him so close. She couldn't stop looking at his mouth, thinking of how it had burned so fiercely against hers.

Mario tipped up her chin so her gaze met his. 'Sabrina?'

She pressed her lips together, trying to keep herself from pitching forward into his arms to finish what they had started. Her body was still aching for him. Every nerve was on high alert for his touch, even her chin felt like fire where his fingers were holding her.

'I didn't want to upset the children,' she finally said.

His brow furrowed. 'The Roebourne children?'

'Yes. They are very young, but not too young to hear what would have been said about their father in the papers if I had told the truth about what had happened.'

Mario released her chin and picked up one of her hands instead, stroking the back of it with his thumb as he held her gaze. 'What did happen?' he asked.

She looked down at her hand in his before bringing her eyes back to his. 'I was very naïve about him,' she said. 'I didn't realise he was grooming me to be his scapegoat. By the time I did realise what was going on it was too late to do anything. The children had enough to deal with, without learning about their father's attempts to seduce me. Besides it was his word against mine. I couldn't see how anyone would believe me.'

Mario's hand tightened around hers. 'Did he threaten you in any way?' he asked.

Her grey eyes became shadowed for a brief moment. 'A couple of times, yes.'

Mario felt his insides burn with bile. He was not a violent man, but right now he wanted to drive his fist into Howard Roebourne's face for how he had maligned Sabrina's reputation. But he was just as angry at himself for treating her the way he had. If he had been thinking with his head instead of other parts of his anatomy he would have realised she couldn't possibly be as bad as she had been portrayed. In spite of her friendship with Laura, Ric would never have agreed to have Sabrina nominated as guardian of Molly if he had not had complete trust in her.

Mario brushed the pad of his thumb across her bottom lip, surprised yet again at how soft her mouth was. A tight little silence pulsed for a beat or two.

'Are you still sore?' he asked hollowly.

She shook her head. 'Please, Mario, don't make a fuss about it. It was my fault for not telling you.'

Mario got to his feet, raking his hand through his hair as he paced the floor. 'Maybe—but if you had told me do you think I would have believed you?' he said in self-disgust. 'I would probably have laughed at you, Sabrina, and carried on regardless.'

'I don't believe that,' she said in a soft voice. 'I don't believe you would have forced me to do anything I didn't want to do.'

He turned to face her, his expression grim. 'I forced you to marry me.'

She gave a little shrug of her slim shoulders. 'For Molly's sake—yes.'

He blew out a breath. 'The thing is, Sabrina, I can't undo what has been done, not yet, at least. You deserve much better than this.'

Sabrina hugged her knees again. 'I'm not sure what you are saying.'

His eyes were very dark as they meshed with hers. 'Why did you let me make love to you earlier this evening?' he asked.

'I'm not sure.' Her teeth sank into her lip again.

'It can not happen again,' he said. 'You do understand that, don't you?'

Sabrina didn't want to examine why her chest suddenly felt so tight. The thorn was back in her throat, making it hard for her to speak past it. 'If that's what you want.'

He muttered a coarse swear-word as he began to pace the floor again. 'What I want is immaterial. Molly needs us both, and we will have to stay married for the time being to keep her out of the clutches of the Knowles, who will no doubt push for custody if we suddenly announce our separation.'

Sabrina could see the sense in what he was saying even though a part of her—the feminine, romantic part of her—was already starting to play with the fanciful scenario of him falling in love with her and asking her to be his wife for real.

Love?

She mentally flinched. Was she in love with him? She had never been in love before but she imagined it would feel exactly like this. Her stomach felt hollow, her heart felt like it was being squeezed between two book-ends and her body was burning for more of his touch.

She chided herself for being so foolish. It was clear he was no longer attracted to her now he knew she was so inexperienced. Some men were like that. They didn't want to spend time tutoring a novice; they would much rather have an experienced lover in their bed. If not his current mistress, no doubt he would find someone else to entertain him during the course of their marriage, maybe even several women. As much as it pained her all she could hope for was that he would be discreet—although that seemed unlikely, given the press's fascination with anything Mario did and who he did it with.

'You are very quiet,' he said. 'Do you not agree we should remain married?'

Sabrina pasted a bland expression on her face. 'I just want to do what is best for Molly.'

'Good,' he said, blowing out a breath. 'That is settled, then.'

Another silence began to suck at the air in the room.

Sabrina held her breath as he came back to where she was sitting on the bed. Her stomach did a crazy little somersault when he brushed the back of his knuckles down the curve of her cheek, his eyes holding hers like the powerful beam of a searchlight. She hoped he couldn't see what she was so desperately trying to hide. If she blurted her feelings to him, now how would he interpret it? He had said at the start he would not take seriously any avowals of love. How she had scoffed at the thought; was it only a day or so ago? What a bitter irony to find herself so deeply in love with him. How had it happened, and so quickly? Was it his deep, dark eyes that had unlocked her heart? Or was it his mouth, the way it kissed her with such potent passion? Or was it the way his touch set fire to her skin, making every pore pucker in excitement?

'I am sorry for hurting you,' he said in a low, deep voice that sounded as if it had been dragged across coarse gravel. 'I will do my best to make it up to you.'

Sabrina could barely get her voice to work. 'You don't have to do anything, Mario.' *Just love me, because I think I'm falling in love with you,* she added silently.

He bent forward and pressed a soft, chaste kiss to the middle of her forehead, making her feel about three years old. '*Buonanotte*, Sabrina,' he said softly.

Sabrina waited until the door had closed behind him before she let out her tightly held breath.

Stupid. Stupid. Stupid.

Over the next few days Sabrina began to see a softening in the housekeeper's attitude towards her. She could only assume Mario had somehow reversed Giovanna's opinion of her as a gold-digger, for the housekeeper had gradually dropped her surliness and had even offered to help Sabrina learn Italian, with limited success.

Sabrina saw very little of Mario, however, just briefly in the mornings when she first got up to tend to Molly and last thing at night when he came home from his office well past dinner. He was polite but distant, asking her about her day and what Molly was up to, but he mentioned nothing personal. It was as if he was building a wall around himself, keeping her on the other side of it. It made her wonder if he had already hooked back up with his model mistress. All the clues were there: the late nights, the slightly ruffled look of his clothes and appearance when he did finally come home, and his stiff formality when speaking to her.

Sabrina constantly berated herself for falling for him. It showed just how naïve she was to have let that one foray into sensuality turn over her heart. He had probably put the whole episode out of his mind by now. He would not be torturing himself over what could have been if things were different between them.

On Friday afternoon while Molly was having a nap Giovanna informed Sabrina there was a delivery of goods for her. 'It is from Signore Marcolini,' she said. 'I think you will be very happy with what he has bought for you.'

Sabrina stood to one side as the courier brought in bag after bag of designer clothes. There were evening dresses, shoes, handbags and evening bags, a range of separates and even some gossamer-fine lingerie. She fingered each item once the courier had left, marvelling at the exquisite fabrics, wondering who Mario had asked for help in selecting such a fabulous wardrobe. While she was grateful for his generosity, she couldn't quite shake off the feeling that he wanted to remodel her into the sort of glamourous wife people would expect a man of his standing to have by his side. Clearly her chain-store clothes and decade-old shoes were not going to cut it. It made her feel tawdry and mousy, like a common sparrow being dressed up as a rare and exotic colourful bird.

'Signore Marcolini will be home early this evening,' Giovanna said when Sabrina came into the salon carrying Molly in her arms later that evening. 'He just called to say he would be here for dinner.'

Sabrina felt another twinge of pique that he hadn't asked to speak to her personally, but pushed it aside to smile at the housekeeper. 'That is nice,' she said. 'Would you like some help with preparing the meal?'

Giovanna looked shocked. '*No, no, no!* I am the house-keeper—you are his wife, *sì*?'

Sabrina put Molly down on the rug so she could kick her little legs. 'You know very well I am not really his wife,' she said with a despondent sigh. 'Not apart from on paper. We don't even share a bedroom.'

Giovanna knelt down beside her to tickle Molly under the chin. 'You are his wife, Signora Marcolini,' she said, still looking at the baby. 'He just does not realise it yet.'

Sabrina turned her head to look at her. 'I think he has a lover,' she said, trying not to choke up.

Giovanna got to her feet in a matter-of-fact manner. 'Rich Italian men often have mistresses,' she said. 'It means nothing.'

'It means something to *me*,' Sabrina returned. 'I don't want to share him with someone else.'

'Perhaps you would not be sharing him with someone

else if you were seeing to his needs yourself,' Giovanna pointed out.

Sabrina felt her cheeks ripen with colour. She turned to look at Molly, and resumed idling playing with her tiny feet. 'We don't have that sort of relationship. It's not what he wants.'

'Has he told you that?'

'Pretty much.'

Giovanna folded her arms across her ample chest. 'I see the way he looks at you, Signora Marcolini. Maybe you need to make the first move, *sì*?'

Sabrina felt herself quake at the thought. What if he rejected her? How would she bear it? She would feel an even bigger fool to have him spurn her clumsy, awkward advances.

'Ah, that is him now,' Giovanna said as the sound of the front door closing echoed through the *palazzo*.

The housekeeper bustled out and within a few moments Mario came in. He reached up to loosen his tie, shrugging himself out of his suit jacket, his smile as he saw Molly kicking and giggling on the floor totally transforming his face. *'Come è il mio piccolo prezioso ragazza?'* he asked, flinging his jacket aside. 'How is my precious little girl?'

Molly cooed at him in delight, kicking her legs all the harder, her tiny starfish hands waving in the air. Mario scooped her up from the floor and kissed her on both cheeks, before turning to face Sabrina. 'Did you get the clothes I sent you?'

Sabrina raised her chin. 'There are lovely. Thank you. You must have spent a fortune.'

He held her gaze for a pulsing moment. 'If you do not like anything in the collection it can always be returned,' he said. 'It will not offend me, I can assure you.'

Pride stiffened her spine a little more. 'I am not used to having someone select my clothes for me.'

He continued to hold her look. 'You are angry, *cara*.'

Sabrina blinked at the endearment, her heart giving a jerky kick of surprise inside her chest. 'No—no, I'm not. It's just I… Some of the things you bought are very personal, and I…'

'Did I get the size right?' he asked before she could finish.

'Yes.' She tucked a strand of hair behind her ear, her face still burning at the thought of those lovely lacy bras and barely there knickers he had chosen for her.

'I have something else for you,' he said. 'It is in my jacket pocket.'

She glanced at his jacket where it was hanging lopsidedly over the back of one of the sofas. 'W-what is it?'

'Go and see.'

Sabrina stepped past him to pick up his jacket. She could feel his body warmth still clinging to it, and his particular male smell. She felt tempted to hold the fabric up to her face to breathe in the essence of him, but stopped herself just in time. Instead she reached inside one of the pockets and found a velvet-covered ring box. She brought it out, her heart thumping wildly as she met his gaze.

'Open it,' he said.

She opened it with careful fingers, her eyes going wide when she saw the two-ring ensemble inside. Diamonds and white gold sparkled back at her brilliantly. She had never seen anything quite so beautiful before. It made her chain-store costume-jewellery collection look like fairground trinkets in comparison.

'Like the clothes, I had to take a guess on your ring size,' he said into the silence. 'If they don't fit the jeweller will adjust them for you.'

Sabrina took the rings out with meticulous care, sliding each one easily over the knuckles of her ring finger.

'They are too loose,' he observed.

'Not by much,' she said, looking up at him shyly.

His eyes held hers for an infinitesimal moment, his expression difficult to read, although his voice when he spoke sounded gruff. 'You are far smaller than I realised. I should have known after the other night.'

She lowered her gaze as she examined the rings on her finger. 'They are truly beautiful.' She looked up at him again. 'I have never had anything quite so beautiful before.'

'I had it specially designed using diamonds from the Marcolini collection.'

Sabrina looked back at the exquisite rings on her finger, thinking wryly of how willingly she had dived into his bed without the lure of priceless diamonds. Was he thinking the same? she wondered as she glanced back at him.

He transferred Molly to his other arm, holding her with casual ease as if he had been taking care of infants all of his life. 'I have made some enquiries about a nanny for Molly,' he said.

Sabrina felt her scalp prickle in apprehension. She feared once a nanny was firmly established in Molly's life there would be no need for her any more. Had the clothes and rings he had given her been part of a consolation prize to make her go away without a fuss?

'Do we need a nanny?' she asked. 'It's not as if I have anything I would rather do with my time.'

Mario cradled Molly's head against his chest with one of his large hands. 'Some of my business associates are keen to meet you.'

'They could meet me here,' she offered. 'We don't have to go out to entertain. I could help Giovanna with the meal. I've done some gourmet cooking courses, and—'

'What is the problem, Sabrina?' he asked, looking at her intently.

Sabrina lowered her gaze again. 'I am not sure I can be all that convincing as a pretend wife. I have the clothes and the rings, but I'm not sure that's really going to be enough to convince anyone.'

'It will have to be enough,' he said, drawing in a breath. 'The press have already announced our union. We will be expected to be out and about like any other recently married couple. I have an important business dinner scheduled for tomorrow evening. People will start to ask questions if you are not there with me.'

She began to twist her hands together. 'But who is going to look after Molly?' she asked. 'We can't leave her with a total stranger.'

'Giovanna will stay overnight,' Mario said. 'She has several grandchildren of her own, so she is used to babies. I am sure she will have no trouble for three or four hours while we are out.'

Sabrina looked at Molly, who had fallen asleep against his broad chest. No wonder the little baby felt so safe and secure in his arms. He was such a big man, tall and strong, and yet surprisingly gentle when the need for it arose. How she longed to feel him touch her again, to tantalise her with his mouth, to captivate her senses until she could think of nothing but how he made her feel. Her body craved him; even now she could feel the pining of her flesh, the nerves so sensitive to his nearness they were making her skin feel too tight for her frame. Her breasts ached for his touch, the graze of his teeth and the sweep of his tongue. Her inner core had stopped hurting days ago, but she missed that tender, intimate reminder of how he had so briefly possessed her. He had been so kind and considerate afterwards, so apologetic it had made it impossible for her not to fall in love with him.

'I think this little girl is ready for bed,' Mario said, carefully handing her back to Sabrina.

She took the sleeping baby from him, her heart racing like a Formula One engine as one of his hands inadvertently brushed against her breast. Her eyes met his for a beat or two before she lowered them to the child in her arms. 'You are very good with her, Mario,' she said. She lifted her gaze back to his. 'She is lucky to have such a wonderful guardian.'

A shadow passed through his dark eyes, like strong sunlight blocked by the passing of thick clouds. 'She would have been much better off with her real parents,' he said. 'There is no substitute for the real thing, is there?'

'No, I guess you are right,' Sabrina said on the back of a sigh. She had often wondered what it would have been like to have a father, especially after her mother had been taken from her when she'd been so young. She had often dreamt of what he would look like, how he would sound and the things he might say to her if they ever met. Why he had not stayed to support her mother she would never know. She had been too young to ask, and now it was too late. When she had seen the words "father unknown" on her birth certificate it had felt like an arrow piercing her heart. It was so hard to accept she didn't belong to anyone. She wondered now if she ever would belong to anyone. Mario had made it pretty clear he was only interested in a temporary arrangement, but how she longed for things to be different.

* * *

When she came back downstairs after putting Molly to bed, Mario was mixing himself a drink at the bar in the salon. He turned as she came into the room. 'Would you like an aperitif?'

'Just tonic water, no gin. Thank you,' she said as she sat on the edge of one of the sofas.

He gave her an ironic look as he handed her the glass of tonic water. 'Keeping a clear head, *cara*?' he asked.

Sabrina took the glass with fingers that felt as if the nerves had been severed. 'Why do you keep calling me that when there is no one around to hear you?'

'Does it bother you?'

She pressed her lips together and looked at the cubes of ice rattling in her glass. 'Not really. It just seems a little unnecessary.'

'I do not find it unnecessary,' he said. 'It is all part of the act, no?'

Sabrina met his satirical gaze. 'How are people ever going to believe you chose someone like me to be your wife?' she asked.

He took a leisurely sip of his drink before he answered. 'You underestimate your charms, Sabrina. You are a very beautiful young woman. I have always thought so, right from the first moment we met.'

She couldn't hold back a churlish retort. 'You thought I was a gold-digger.'

His mouth momentarily tightened. 'And I was wrong. I have apologised, Sabrina. I can do no more.'

She crossed her legs, cradling her drink in both hands in case she spilt it. 'If you thought I was so beautiful, why did you feel the need to revamp my wardrobe?'

His eyes warred with hers for a tense moment. 'I can see that has become somewhat of an issue with you,' he said. 'Believe it or not, I was trying to help you. I would imagine it is not easy shopping with a small infant in tow. But, since you don't appreciate the gesture, I will have everything taken back. I will arrange for you to have your own credit card with maximum credit.'

Sabrina felt sudden tears thicken her throat as he turned away from her to refresh his drink. The tension in his back and shoulders made her regret her childish response to his act of thoughtfulness. 'I'm sorry,' she said softly. 'It was wrong of me to be so ungrateful. I realise you were only trying to be helpful.'

Mario turned to face her. 'You are not used to people being kind to you, are you, *tesore mio*?'

Sabrina brushed at her prickling eyes with the back of her hand. 'I'm sorry for being so…so emotional right now.'

He put down his drink and came over to where she was sitting, hunkering down in front of her like he would a small child. His eyes were soft as they held hers, his fingers as he stroked her tear-stained cheek even softer. 'You are not the one who should be apologising for anything, Sabrina,' he said. 'We have both been through a dreadful time. It is to be expected that we will have shifts of mood in these early days and months of grief.'

'I know.' She gave a deep, shuddering sigh. 'I know…'

Mario traced a fingertip over her trembling bottom lip. Again he was amazed at how soft and pillowy her mouth was. He ached to feel it under his, but he knew where it would lead if he kissed her again. She had affected him much more than he had realised; that bittersweet taste of her had left him wanting in a way he had never wanted before. His body throbbed to feel her moist warmth again, but she was shy and hesitant around him, and he could hardly blame her for it. He had treated her appallingly. He loathed recalling some of the things he had said to her; doing so made his guilt all the harder to bear. He had done his best to make it up to her, but she seemed to be offended no matter what he did. Most women would have been mollified with gifts of jewellery and designer clothes, but she had turned her freckled, *re-troussé* nose up at them.

He had lain awake the last few nights thinking of how he had hurt her. She was so petite, it tortured him to think of what damage he might have done. He had brutalised her in his savage desire for satiation, arrogantly assuming she was with him all the way when she had probably not even been aware of what she had been doing, nor what she had been communicating. Her instincts had taken over and he had exploited them.

'You have such a soft mouth,' he said. 'Do you realise I have never seen you smile at me?'

She gave him a tentative half-smile. 'Really?'

He smiled back. 'Really.'

She shifted her gaze from his, her mouth turning down at the corners. 'I guess I haven't had all that much to smile about just lately.'

Mario got to his feet and, taking one of her hands, pulled her up to stand in front of him. He slid his hands down the length of her arms, relishing the silky feel of her smooth skin, his groin tightening in response. He held himself away from her, not wanting to reveal how turned on he was in case she was frightened. She looked up at him with her clear grey eyes, and he felt something move inside his chest, like a lever being shifted to a position it had never been in before.

The silence swelled and swelled, making the air thick, heavy and drugging.

Mario's gaze went to her mouth, his heart rate picking up its pace as he saw her moisten her lips with the tip of her tongue. He felt the blood surge in his veins, the primal urge to feel her against his hardness too much for him to withstand. He muttered a short, sharp imprecation and then lowered his mouth to hers.

CHAPTER NINE

SABRINA melted against him as his kiss deepened, the movement of his tongue against hers unlocking every vertebra of her spine. Her legs felt woolly, and her belly did crazy zigzags, like a Buick on black ice, as his hands found the small of her back and pressed her up close to his erection. Her body burned at the intimate contact; it felt like flames were leaping beneath her skin, scorching her in every secret place. The feminine heart of her began to ache with an on-off pulse, a deep, throbbing ache that she knew instinctively no one could ever satisfy but him.

His kiss became more and more urgent as she laced her arms around his neck, his tongue calling hers into a fast-paced tango. Electric sensations danced along her skin, her chest wall reverberating with the pounding of her racing heart.

He tasted so fresh and so arrantly male, his unshaven skin scraping her tender face as he angled his head to change position. The kiss this time was slower, tantalisingly so. Sabrina could feel herself being swept away on a sensual tide of longing so intense she felt as if her body had completely taken over her mind. There was no room for rational thought, her body had already decided what it wanted and was doing everything in its power to communicate it to him. She nipped at his bottom lip with her teeth, gently, playfully, teasingly, until he growled deep in his throat and did the same to her. Shivers cascaded down her spine as his strong white teeth captured her kiss-swollen lip, his tongue sweeping over it before his teeth made her his slave again.

Sabrina felt his hands move from her lower back to skate up her sides, resting just beneath the gentle swell of her breasts. Her nipples tingled in excitement, the puckered flesh pressing against the lace of her bra, desperate for the hot, sweet suck of his mouth and the lick and glide of his raspy male tongue.

She gave a little whimper when his thumbs brushed over her, his mouth still commandeering hers. Her heart thundered in her chest, the drum beat of her pulse roaring in her ears like the tumultuous waves of a wild ocean.

Mario lifted his mouth from hers and looked down at her with eyes blazing with desire. 'This might be a good time to stop,' he said. 'Before things get out of hand.'

Sabrina's body felt cold and unstable without the solid prop of his. His hands were now holding her by the upper arms, but she longed for the hot press of his body against hers. She swallowed the ropey lump of disappointment in her throat, her spirits wilting at the realisation of how easy it was for him to release her. His desire for her was a transient, controllable thing, unlike hers, which had reduced her almost to the point of begging.

'I suppose your mistress might not be too happy about you sleeping with your wife as well as her.' She spoke her thoughts out loud.

His eyes studied hers. It seemed a decade before he spoke.

'You know, for a moment there I thought you sounded jealous.'

Sabrina felt her colour rise but raised her chin regardless. 'I don't want to be laughed at by everyone.'

'No one is laughing at you, *cara mia*.'

Tears burned like acid at the back of her eyes. 'Stop calling me that,' she said, desperately trying to control the wobble of her chin. 'Please don't make fun of me. I can't bear it.'

Mario's hands moved from her upper arms to encircle her wrists, his fingers overlapping each other. 'What is this about, Sabrina? What is it *really* about?'

Her throat moved up and down as if she was shuffling through the words before she spoke them. 'I'm not sure…'

'Look at me.'

She slowly raised her eyes to his, her bottom lip quivering ever so slightly.

'I do not have a mistress right now,' he said.

Her pupils went wide, like black saucers. 'Y-you don't?'

He gave her a rueful smile. 'No, *tesore mio*. But perhaps it would be a good idea if I did, for then I would not be so tempted to sleep with you.'

She licked her blood-red lips with a quick dart-like movement of her tongue. 'You're…' She swallowed again. 'You're…tempted? Really?'

He stroked the undersides of her small wrists with the pads of his thumbs, watching as her whole body reacted. He felt her faint shiver, saw the way the grey pools of her eyes darkened, and the way her pulse leapt and fluttered beneath his touch. 'I am sorely tempted, but I swore I would not touch you again,' he said. 'A promise is a promise, even if it was only to myself.'

There was a pregnant pause.

'What if…?' She moistened her mouth again before continuing, 'What if I wanted you to sleep with me?'

Mario drew in a long breath, holding it for a few beats before releasing it, along with her wrists. He put some distance between them, dragging a hand through his hair, searching for patience, strength, resolve. 'Sabrina…you don't know what you are asking.'

'I think I do,' she said quietly.

He looked at her again, his heart feeling as if a clamp was pressing the sides together. It seemed strange to him how young she seemed now, when only weeks ago he had thought her so streetwise and worldly. How could he have been so blind? She was so innocent; she didn't know what the hell she was getting in to by asking him to be her lover. She was vulnerable and sweet, and he would be a cad to have a short-term 'affair' with her. She wasn't the affair type. 'Sabrina…' He finger-combed his hair again. '*Cara*, listen to me.'

Her limpid eyes began to glisten. 'It's all right,' she said stiffly, turning her back to him as she moved to the other side of the room. 'I understand, really I do. I'm not your type. You've made it clear right from the start.'

Mario swore in both English and Italian, a perverse part of him pleased at how she flinched as the words cut the air. 'For God's sake, Sabrina, you are still in my mind a virgin.'

'I wasn't aware it was something to be ashamed of.'

'Of course it's nothing to be ashamed of,' he said. 'You should be proud of it, especially in this day and age.'

She turned to look at him. 'If you don't mind, I think I will give dinner a miss. I'm not hungry.'

Mario swore again, this time under his breath. 'Sulking is for small children, Sabrina.'

She put her chin up at him. 'You think I'm in a sulk?'

'I think you are young and vulnerable and in way over your head, *tesore mio*,' he said, with a crooked smile to soften the words.

She set her mouth so tightly he could see brackets of strain around the soft lips he had kissed only minutes ago. 'I guess I'll see you in the morning,' she said, her shoulders slumping as she made to move past.

Mario placed one of his hands on the cup of her shoulder, holding her in place. 'Don't run away, Sabrina,' he said gently. 'Stay with me. Talk to me.'

Her bottom lip trembled slightly and her white, even teeth sank down to steady it. Her eyes skittered away from his, her cheeks flushed with colour.

Mario cupped the nape of her neck with his palm, his fingers tangling in her silky hair, tying her to him. 'Look at me, Sabrina,' he commanded again, softly this time.

She raised her eyes to his, her tone short and self-deprecating. 'I'm sorry for embarrassing you. But I guess you must be pretty used to women falling all over themselves to sleep with you.'

He brushed his thumb over the pouting protrusion of her bottom lip. 'Firstly, I am not at all embarrassed, and secondly, I do not have as many women in my life as you might think. If I did everything the press said I did, I would not have any time for my work.'

Her eyes moved away from his again. 'You say you don't have a current mistress, but I'm guessing it won't be long before you do.'

Mario studied her features for a long moment. She had lilac thumbprint-like shadows beneath her eyes, and her brow was networked with fine lines of uncertainty. He had become so used to a certain arrogant confidence in all his previous partners, he had not thought anything of it until now. Now all he wanted was the shy innocence of Sabrina. He ached for it—for her hesitant touch, for her sweet-but-feverish kisses and the feminine pulse of her body against his. He wanted to claim her as his, to tutor her in the wild, secret world of her sensuality, to fill her with his hardness, to spill himself as she convulsed around him. His body leapt at the thought, his blood rocketing through his veins, surging to his loins until he was throbbing with need.

He clenched his teeth, fighting the temptation, but it was impossible to ignore the magnetic pull of her body so close to his.

'Is…is everything all right?' she asked in a voice so soft he had to strain to hear it.

'No,' he said gruffly as he took her by the hips and pulled her up against him.

Her eyes flared as she felt him. 'I—I thought you said—?'

'Forget what I said,' he growled as he bent his head to hers. 'Forget the hell what I said.'

Sabrina stifled a gasp as his mouth seared hers, the hot urgency of it sweeping her up into a maelstrom of heady sensation. Desire licked along her veins like a river of fire, lightning-fast, lightning-hot and equally electrifying. His fingers dug into her hips, holding her tighter against his hot, hard need. Her body quivered at the intimate contact, the outline of his erection making her legs weaken.

His mouth continued its sensual assault, his tongue stroking and stabbing at hers simultaneously, drawing her into a whirlpool of wanting that was uncontrollable. Her tongue danced with his, darting and diving to evade, and then licking and stroking to cajole. He responded by kissing her harder and deeper, his lower body grinding against hers as the pressure built.

His hands moved from her hips to slide up her ribcage and possess her breasts, the warm cup of his palms making the pores of her flesh stand up in goose bumps of excitement. Her spine felt as if it had been injected with warm, smooth honey, her limbs equally malleable, as his mouth moved from hers to the scaffold of her collarbone. She shivered as his lips whispered over her sensitive skin, every nerve arching its back to feel more of his touch.

'I told myself I wasn't going to do this,' he said. 'I *promised* myself.'

Sabrina felt another shiver dance over her skin as his lips moved against her neck when he spoke. 'It's all right,' she said on a breathless gasp. 'I'm a big girl now.'

He brushed her mouth with a hard, possessive kiss, his dark eyes hooded and brooding. 'I'm afraid I'll hurt you again.'

Sabrina felt his erection thick and swollen against her, making her insides melt like candle wax. 'You won't hurt me,' she whispered against his mouth. 'I am sure you won't.'

He kissed her again, deeply and lingeringly, exploring every contour of her mouth before he moved his lips to the breast he had deftly uncovered. His mouth closed over one puckered nipple, sucking on her hungrily, before he circled her with his tongue. Pleasure ricocheted through her like gunfire, piercing the sound barrier. Waves of feeling washed over her, tossing her about until she was clinging to him like a raft.

'We need to go upstairs,' he said, and lifted her off her feet.

'Put me down,' Sabrina protested. 'I'm too heavy.'

'You weigh next to nothing,' he said, and carried her out of the room and up the sweeping staircase.

Sabrina linked her arms around his neck, her belly feeling as if a hundred tiny fists were trying to punch their way out. She breathed in his scent; the exotic spices of his aftershave mixed with the essence of his maleness made her nostrils flare in excitement. Nervousness and anticipation were jostling for position inside her, making her feel dizzy and light-headed at the thought of finally being possessed by him. Her body was preparing itself, the moist dew of desire already secretly anointing her, the deep throb of her inner core like a low, deep drum-beat.

Mario shouldered open his bedroom-suite door, kicking it shut with his foot once they were inside. He let her slide down his body as he set her down, his eyes searing hers with passionate promise. 'Are you sure this is what you want?' he asked. 'It's not too late to change your mind.'

Sabrina snatched in a scratchy breath. 'I want you, Mario. I want you to make love to me.'

His gaze darkened to a black, bottomless pool of desire. 'I wanted you the moment I met you,' he said as he walked her backwards to the bed, slowly, inexorably.

'I—I know,' she said shakily, her thighs bumping against his.

He ran his hands down her arms, entrapping her wrists as her knees came up against the mattress. There was a primitive element to his hold, a heated charge of energy she could feel passing from his body to hers. His body simmered with it; hers felt like it was boiling.

He slowly undressed her, kissing her flesh as it was revealed to him until she was standing in just her bra and knickers, her skin tingling wherever his lips had burned and branded her as his. 'Now you get to undress me,' he said with a smouldering look that lifted every hair on her scalp.

Sabrina's fingers fumbled with the buttons on his shirt, but somehow she got them undone. She tugged it out of his trousers and slid it off his broad shoulders, pausing to kiss his bronzed flesh, tasting the saltiness of him, relishing in the feel of his sculptured muscles under the soft press of her fingertips. Her lips brushed against his hard, flat nipples, her tongue sweeping and curling over him, her belly turning over in excitement when he groaned in pleasure.

Her fingers came to the waistband of his trousers. She glanced up at him shyly, wondering if she had the courage to follow through. His eyes glittered darkly with expectation, and she took a shallow breath and unhooked his belt from its buckle, slowly pulling it through until it dropped to the floor with a serpent-like slither.

'You are in control, Sabrina,' Mario said, although it sounded rough and uneven. 'Any time you want to stop, you stop.'

Sabrina traced the pathway of masculine hair from his belly button to his waistband with her fingers, delighting in the taut flatness of his abdomen, the ridged muscles contracting even more at her touch. 'I don't want to stop,' she said lightly, skating her fingertips over the tenting of his trousers.

She heard him suck in a harsh breath, his body whipcord-tight as she continued stroking him, exploring the length and breadth of him through the barrier of his clothes.

One of his hands came over hers, holding her against him as he fought for control. 'Give me a moment,' he bit out.

Sabrina looked up at him in alarm. 'Am I doing something wrong?'

'No, *cara*,' he said, shuddering as her fingers moved against him. 'I am getting a little ahead of myself, that is all.'

Her hand stilled but she could still feel him throbbing against her palm. He was so magnificently male, so magnificently aroused. She moved her fingers experimentally, feeling him, shaping him, and then, with a swiftly indrawn breath for courage, she unzipped him.

He stepped out of his trousers, his black underwear the only remaining barrier. Sabrina's fingers danced over him, and then with increasing boldness she peeled back the stretchy black fabric and exposed the proud length of him.

She saw the muscles of his abdomen clench in preparation for her first skin-on-skin touch, the pearl-like bead of moisture at his blunt tip making her stomach free-fall.

She ran her fingertip down him from shaft to tip, amazed at how silky his taut skin felt. He was satin-covered steel, sexual energy still leashed but visibly straining. She felt the latent power of him against her curling fingers; she felt too the deep all-over shudder he gave as her hand finally enclosed him.

'My turn, I think,' he said, and captured her hand.

The look in his eyes made her stomach drop another fifty floors. He turned her hand over and kissed the middle of her palm, his tongue circling it, teasing the sensitive nerves, until they were screaming for mercy beneath her skin.

His other hand moved to the small of her back, sliding upwards until he came to the clasp of her bra. She pulled in an uneven breath as it fell to the floor with a lacy silence.

His eyes consumed her greedily, taking in her small-but-neat, creamy-white form, the rosy-red nipples already pert and aching for his lips and tongue. He bent his head and suckled on her, taking his time over each breast, torturing her with his caresses until she was clutching at his shoulders, panting breathlessly.

'You are so dainty and yet so perfect,' he said against the satin smoothness of her right breast, his lips making the tender flesh shiver in reaction.

Sabrina couldn't speak when his mouth closed over her nipple again. She felt the rough glide of his tongue over her, the moist heat of his mouth making her whimper in pleasure.

His hands settled on her hips, holding her against his arousal with just the fragile cobweb of her lacy knickers between his body and hers. He nudged against her experimentally, his eyes smoky as they held hers. 'It is still not too late to stop,' he said. 'You are still in control, Sabrina. Always remember that—you are the one in control.'

Sabrina felt her heart give an almighty squeeze that was almost painful. He was being so tender and considerate; how could she not love him? She wanted to tell him, but held back just in time. He had not given any indication of feeling anything but lust for her. Why spoil the moment with confessions of a love that had no future? She was only in his life because of his guardianship of Molly. His physical desire for her was a bonus, a temporary diversion, until he moved on to his next mistress.

His reputation said it all. Yes, the papers whipped it up a bit, but even so it was obvious he was a no-strings-sex guy. He liked to play and to play hard. Sabrina was a novelty to him, a naïve innocent who made a stark change from the worldly, streetwise women he normally bedded. But it wouldn't matter how experienced she became; Sabrina knew Mario was the only man who could make her feel the way she was currently feeling. No one else had kissed her until she was senseless. No one else had made her ache with a need so strong she felt as if her breathing was going to stop altogether unless he assuaged it.

'Touch me, Mario,' she whispered as she leant into his hardness.

He moved his hand down to cup her through the lace, her intimate dampness making his pupils dilate. 'You are beautiful,' he said, low and deep.

With him touching her like that, Sabrina *felt* beautiful. She felt powerful, too, full of feminine power to attract a mate. She moved against his hand, her body thrilling at the contact, her feminine flesh quivering. His fingers moved aside the lace of her knickers to trace her moist cleft, gently separating her before he slowly inserted one finger. She gasped at the sensation of feeling him move inside her, exploring her tenderly, preparing her for the ultimate possession of his body.

After a moment he guided her down onto the bed. 'Relax, *cara*,' he said as he came down beside her, his long legs entwining with hers. 'Don't tense up on me.'

Sabrina tried to loosen up, but every nerve in her body seemed to be switched to hyper-vigilance mode. She wanted him so badly she felt twitchy and restless, feverish with excitement and escalating need. She arched her spine as he peeled away her underwear, her breathing coming in ever-shortening intervals as his hand came back to cup her.

'You are so very tempting.'

Sabrina shivered as his fingers explored her again, stretching her to accommodate him. Her muscles fought him at first, but he kissed her to distract her, and after a moment he went deeper.

It wasn't enough. It wasn't what she wanted. She wanted *him*, deep and hot and hard, inside her.

She pulled his hand away and nestled closer, touching him, squeezing her fingers around his length. He bit back a groan and lay back, propped up on his elbows while she caressed him, his laboured breathing making his chest rise and fall like a pair of bellows. 'I am going to come if you don't stop that,' he said through tightly clenched teeth.

'I would like to see you,' Sabrina said, surprising herself at her boldness.

'Not this time,' he said, and flipped her on to her back. 'We'll save that for another time. This time it is all about you.'

Sabrina watched as he opened the bedside-table drawer to retrieve a condom. Again she had to push aside the thought of how many other women had lain on this bed with him; this was not the time to reflect on his past. This was her time with him, a time to enjoy the pleasure of her body under the tutelage of his. And her body was enjoying it. It was pulsing with longing, quaking all over with it, as she watched him roll the condom over his erection.

He moved over her to kiss her mouth lingeringly, teasing her with his tongue, the stab and thrusting action mimicking the intimate union that was to come.

Sabrina made room for him between her legs, her heart giving a little jump of exhilaration as he brushed her moist entrance.

'Not so fast, *cara*,' he chided her gently as he pulled back. 'There are things I have to do first.'

A small frown tugged at her brow. 'What things?'

He gave her a smouldering look. 'These things,' he said, and kissed his way from her breasts over her quivering belly until he got to the dark, neatly trimmed curls that shielded the secret heart of her.

Sabrina stopped breathing when his mouth separated her, his tongue sending electric pulses of sensations to her curling toes and back. Her back lifted off the bed as he intensified the movement of his caressing tongue, all the delicious feelings seeming to gather at one tight point, hovering there, waiting for the final moment to explode.

'Go with it, *cara*,' he coaxed her gently. 'Don't fight it. Let go.'

She couldn't believe her body could contain so much feeling as the first waves rolled over her, lifting her up higher and higher, until she was spinning in a vortex of sensation. Spasm after spasm rocketed through her, making her aware of nothing but her body and how Mario had made it feel. Her limbs felt deliciously loose, the lassitude of physical release flowing through her like a warm tide.

He slowly moved back up her body, stroking her, caressing her, until she felt the need building again. She moved against him, aching for the primal connection of their bodies.

'Please,' she said, beyond caring that she was almost begging. '*Please…*'

'Don't be impatient, *mio piccolo*,' he growled playfully as he positioned himself, a leg over one of hers, an intimate tangle of limbs. 'I am trying to be careful with you, but you are making it almost impossible for me to slow down.'

Sabrina felt him at her entrance, the heat of him just hovering there making her breath hitch in her throat. 'I don't want you to slow down,' she said, clutching at his shoulders. 'I want to feel you…all of you.'

He kissed her on the mouth, lingering there before he

pushed in slowly, just the tip, waiting until she accepted him before going further. 'Tell me if I am hurting you,' he said against her lips.

'You're not hurting me,' she breathed back, her lips tingling from the movement of his own against their sensitive surface.

He thrust a little deeper, gauging her response, waiting until she stretched before he moved again. 'You feel so good,' he said in a deep, throaty tone. 'So unbelievably good.'

Sabrina felt the stirring of her senses as he moved more deeply within her, the pleasure he was feeling evident by the contorted expression on his face as he fought for control. She ran her hands over his back and shoulders, delighting in the feel of him teetering on the edge of release. So much power, so much strength, and yet he was so tender with her. The love she felt for him swelled in her chest, taking up so much room she could barely breathe without feeling like she was snagging on something deep inside.

Mario slowly built his pace, the tantalising friction sending Sabrina's senses into another wheel-spin. Instinct told her he was getting closer and closer to the point of no return. She could feel the tension in his body, the way his breathing became more hectic, and the way his hold on her subtly tightened.

She wriggled beneath him, arching her back like a sinuous cat, wanting that final trigger to make her pleasure complete.

He delved between their rocking bodies, stroking her swollen dampness until she plunged headfirst into the abyss of paradise, her body shaking, convulsing and twitching as he emptied himself in a series of hard pumps that left her breathless and gasping.

Sabrina listened to the sound of his breathing for a long time without moving. Her body felt boneless, her senses so satiated she could barely tie two thoughts together in her head.

'Am I too heavy for you?' Mario asked after what seemed an extraordinarily long time.

'No. You feel…nice.'

'Nice is not a word usually used to describe me,' he said wryly as he rolled away.

Sabrina felt the cooler air rush at her like an icy slap on the face. He was distancing himself. There had been no loving aftermath, no lingering over a final kiss or two. There had been a long silence, and then…nothing. Was he regretting sleeping with her? Or had she not pleased him the way he normally expected a woman to please him?

He had done this a thousand times, she reminded herself. It was nothing special. This was not an experience that would live in his memory as it would hers. She was a fill-in, an amusing diversion while they were shackled together for the sake of a small child.

'I need to check on Molly,' she said, and clutching at the sheet, used it like a wrap to cover her nakedness as she got off the bed.

'Is the baby monitor not working?' he asked.

Sabrina pressed her lips together as she glanced at the device he had installed in every room. 'Yes, but it doesn't hurt to look in on her,' she said. 'Sometimes she wriggles out from beneath the covers.'

There was still nothing in his expression to indicate the intimacy they had just shared, or even if he had been affected by it. 'I will check on her while you get dressed for dinner,' he said, tying the ends of his bathrobe firmly around his waist.

'Giovanna has gone to a lot of trouble. I would hate to disappoint her.'

Sabrina flinched as the door clicked shut on his exit; all things considered, it seemed a rather fitting punctuation-mark on her hopes.

CHAPTER TEN

MARIO was on his second drink when Sabrina came into the dining room half an hour later. She brought the fresh fragrance of summer flowers with her, a light, carefree scent that teased his nostrils. She had pulled her still-damp hair up into a pony-tail-cum-knot that looked both casual and elegant, and her face was lightly made up, her lips shining with lip gloss. Her eyes, however, were not quite making the distance to his.

He wasn't sure what else he had been expecting. He wasn't even sure if he had a right to expect anything. He suspected she had wanted to sleep with him more out of a sense of adventure than anything else. Now it was over with, she was regretting it. He didn't regret making love with her, not for a moment, it was more that by doing so he felt he had crossed a boundary and now he couldn't uncross it. He had travelled into unchartered territory; the feelings he was experiencing were foreign to him. He hardly knew what to make of them.

He had slept with lots of women in the past, and not one of them had left a lasting impression on his senses. And yet his body was still humming from making love with Sabrina earlier. His skin had lifted in a frisson of excitement as soon as she'd walked into the room. He felt the tension building in him as each second ticked past, the roar of his blood, the tightening of his flesh and the ache in his loins.

He put the gossip magazine he had been flicking through aside, wondering if Sabrina had seen the photographs of him carrying Molly at the airport on the day of their arrival in Rome. The caption had read: *high-flying playboy now a tamed family man*. It had shocked him a little to see himself portrayed in such a domestic way. It made him think longingly of his freedom, of the come-and-go lifestyle he had always taken for granted. There would be compensations, he knew. Molly was an engaging infant, and would no doubt grow into a beautiful child. He owed it to Ric to concentrate on giving Molly the most secure and happy childhood he could. The other compensation of course was Sabrina—but he wasn't so sure he wanted to linger too long on what to make of his ambiguous feelings where she was concerned.

'Would you care for a drink?' Mario asked, to break the silence.

Her lips moved in the semblance of a smile, but it was fleeting; it disappeared as soon as her eyes met his. 'Thank you. White wine, if you have it.'

Mario poured her a glass of chilled white wine and handed it to her wryly, noting how her hand shook slightly as she took it from him. 'There is no need to be nervous, Sabrina.'

Her eyes skittered away from his. 'I'm not nervous.'

He picked up his glass and twirled the contents, the sound of the ice cubes bumping against the sides loud in the silence.

'I would like to talk to you about our future,' he said.

Her finely arched brows lifted, making her grey eyes larger than a startled fawn's. 'I see…'

'Actually, I don't think you do,' Mario said, putting his glass down.

Her chin rose a little, although she sneaked in a quick lick of her lips which totally belied her cool composure. 'I understand this arrangement between us is temporary,' she said. 'I also understand that a marriage of convenience is only workable if it is convenient to both parties.'

'In our case it is convenient for three parties,' Mario pointed out. 'Molly needs both of us.'

'Yes, but you said—'

'I have changed my mind.'

She stepped backwards as if he had slapped her. 'W-what?'

'I have changed my mind about how long our marriage should continue.' He paused for a beat or two before adding, 'I would like it to continue indefinitely.'

He watched as her throat moved up and down, the motion like a small mouse wriggling under a blanket. Her tongue came out again, a quick flash of movement across her lips, her eyes flickering with alarm. 'But you don't… I mean, we don't love each other,' she said.

Mario leaned back against the bar, crossing one ankle over the other as he held her gaze.

'Any marriage is a bit of a gamble,' he said, uncrossing his ankles and straightening to his full height. 'But, when two people are prepared to make it work, it can be very satisfying in the long term.'

'What about love?' she whispered

'Sabrina, we have a chance to make this work for Molly's sake,' he said. 'I believe it is the best thing for her to have two parents who live together in companionship if nothing else.'

Sabrina felt her stomach clench in despair. 'But what about

what I want?' she asked. 'I want children of my own. How can I have the family I've always wanted if I am tied indefinitely to you?'

He held her questioning look for a pulsing moment before he shifted his gaze. He sent his hand through his hair and moved to the other side of the room. 'I do not want to have children,' he said. 'I am sorry, but that is not something I have ever seen for myself. The responsibility of Molly is more than enough for me.'

She stared at him in bewilderment. 'You're expecting me to give up that lifelong dream for you?'

His eyes came back to hers, hot, hard and determined. 'Not for me—for Molly,' he said. 'If it is too much to ask you to sacrifice having children, then after a suitable time I will release you from our marriage.'

Sabrina felt her stomach fold over in panic. 'Define "a suitable time".'

His eyes moved away from hers again. 'I can't put an exact time on it. It will depend on many things.'

She lifted her chin. 'Like my turning a blind eye to what you do on the side?' she asked.

His expression tightened. 'If you are not happy with the conditions, you know what you can do. You will be more than adequately compensated.'

She put her wine glass down and brushed back her hair with an unsteady hand. 'I'm not sure what has motivated this,' she said. 'But if it has anything to do with what happened earlier, I—'

'It has everything to do with what happened earlier.'

Sabrina rolled her lips together, her eyes hunting his for a sign of what he was feeling, but his expression was as neutral as if they had been discussing the weather. 'Wow, I must have really impressed you in bed!' She affected an airy tone.

A smile flashed through his dark eyes. 'You did.'

'The novelty factor, right?'

'Wrong.'

She stopped breathing as he closed the distance between them. Her heart began to hammer as his hands settled about her waist, his long fingers warm and strong as he brought her that little bit closer. She felt the stirring of his body against her, the slow and steady burn of his gaze making her toes curl up inside her shoes. Her eyes flicked to his mouth, his sexy half-smile sending another hot rush of liquid longing between her thighs.

He brought one hand up to her face, cupping her cheek as he brushed the pad of his thumb over her lips in a caress that was as gentle as it was potent. She felt every sensitive nerve snap to attention, each one buzzing with expectation.

When he touched her like this it was all too easy to put aside her hopes and dreams to have another moment of magic in his arms. But Sabrina wondered how long it would be before she began to resent him, to hate him for holding her back, for not allowing her to access his heart. He was not willing to give up his freedom. That hurt, so too did the fact that he would never commit to her emotionally. Why else would he refuse to blend his blood with hers and have a child together? That was the biggest slap in the face of all—he didn't want any permanent reminders of their liaison. Molly was enough responsibility for him; dear, little motherless Molly, who would very likely be the one to get hurt in the long run when her guardians were eventually torn apart with bitterness and recrimination.

Sabrina pulled out of his hold, rubbing at her arms as if her skin was itchy from a rash. 'Don't do this, Mario,' she said. 'This is not how normal people behave.'

'What is normal about our situation?' he asked. 'We have been thrown together by circumstances beyond our control. I think it is up to us to make the best of the hand we have been dealt.'

'I don't know about how you live your life, but mine is not and never has been a game,' Sabrina shot back with a glare.

He let out a breath as he raked his fingers through his hair. 'I am not suggesting we treat this lightly. I am sorry if I have given you that impression. Having a child is a big step. It is too big a step for me. I watched my brother and his wife go through a painful separation after the loss of their first baby. I am the first to admit there are no guarantees, but I want this to work, Sabrina. I want it to work for Molly, but also for Ric and Laura. They chose us for a reason. Think about it for a moment—they must have been confident we could make a go of it as a couple, otherwise they would never have nominated us.'

She threw her hands in the air. 'I've thought about it, Mario, and I still can't believe they did what they did. We are polar opposites. If we had met under any other circumstances, you wouldn't have given me a second glance.'

'You underestimate yourself, *cara*,' he said. 'You are one of the most beautiful women I have ever met. But unlike a lot of other women I know you don't choose to display it at every opportunity.'

She rolled her eyes and swung away again. 'You only want me because of my inexperience. It's a primal thing; it has nothing to do with emotion, but everything to do with evolution.'

'I admit that I find your innocence refreshing,' he said. 'But it is not just about that. There are many things I like about you.'

Sabrina pursed her lips as she waited for him to continue.

'I like the fact that you let the public think what they wanted over the Roebourne affair in order to protect the children,' he said. 'I also like the fact that you agreed to marry me even though you disliked me intensely. Once again, you put your feelings aside for the sake of a small child. Those are very admirable qualities, *cara*.'

She let out a small sigh. 'I don't really dislike you intensely—at least, not now.'

His expression contained a hint of wryness. 'I kind of figured that.'

Sabrina wondered what else he had figured out. Did he know how much she loved him? Was he laughing at her naivety for falling for a man who had no intention of returning that love? Although he said he wanted their marriage to continue indefinitely, he had spoken of *liking* her—not loving her. There was a very big difference, and it mattered to her. It mattered a great deal. How could she settle for second best when all her life she had dreamed of having it all—a man who adored her, a child or two to cement that love? Bringing up their little family as a solid unit, the sort of unit she had been denied during her childhood.

The loneliness of her upbringing had always tormented her. That was why she had married Mario; to protect Molly from experiencing the same—or at least it had been one of the reasons. He could have looked like the proverbial bell-ringer at Notre Dame and she still would have married him to protect her little god-daughter—although it was rather a bonus that he didn't, she thought as her eyes went to his again. He was the most amazingly good-looking man; her heart fluttered every time she looked at him. Would she still feel this way in two, ten or even twenty years? Or would she end up hating him for locking her into a loveless marriage that existed only for the sake of Molly?

She shifted her weight, forcing her eyes to make the full distance to his penetrating gaze. 'Just because we…had sex doesn't mean I am in love with you.'

'It would be hypocritical of me to expect you to be,' he returned. 'I have had sex with many women without once falling in love.'

Sabrina tried to ignore the spike of jealousy that jabbed at her at his statement. 'Women you will continue to sleep with?' she asked.

His eyes never once moved away from hers. 'I told you before, I expect our marriage to be an exclusive arrangement.'

She cocked a finely arched brow at him. 'You mean you won't keep a mistress on the side?'

'Why would I want a mistress when I have you to warm my bed?' he asked with a look that smouldered like hot coals.

Sabrina felt her breath catch inside her chest. 'So…so you want our marriage to be a normal one, but without actually falling in love with each other?'

He studied her for a pregnant pause, not speaking, barely even moving.

Sabrina supposed that was his answer: no answer. He was not prepared to commit himself emotionally. He had never been in love with any of his lovers, why should she be any different? Why torture herself with foolish hopes that would only break her heart in the end?

'Signore and Signora Marcolini?' Giovanna's voice sounded from the doorway. '*La cena è pronta.*'

'*Grazie*, Giovanna,' Mario answered. 'Dinner is ready,' he translated for Sabrina.

She followed him to the elegantly laid-out table, sitting down on the chair he pulled out for her. 'Thank you.'

'My brother and sister-in-law are keen to meet you,' he said once he had taken the seat opposite. 'Remember the business dinner I mentioned?'

'The one tomorrow evening?'

'Yes,' he said, spreading his napkin across his lap. 'As joint heirs to our father's estate, Antonio tries to attend most of the bigger functions, although he leaves most of the business end of things to me due to his surgical commitments. He and Claire will be there tomorrow. They have just returned from abroad. He called me while you were having a shower.'

Sabrina toyed with the rings on her finger before meeting his gaze. 'What sort of business is it that you do?'

'Corporate lending and fund management,' he answered. 'I also have a commercial-property portfolio that I run on the side. Lots of eggs in lots of baskets.'

'It sounds very demanding.'

'It is, but then I have always liked a challenge.'

Sabrina shifted her gaze from his glinting eyes, her fingers moving from her ring to fiddle with her soup spoon instead. 'I suppose you treat everything in life, including women like me, as a challenge to be conquered.'

He reached across the table to capture her hand, bringing it up to his mouth, his eyes holding hers as he pressed a ghost of a kiss to her bent knuckles. 'You, *tesore mio*, have been a delightful challenge,' he said. 'I have enjoyed every minute of it.'

Sabrina pulled her hand out of his and tucked it away from

temptation in her lap. 'I need some time to think about the no-children issue.' She took an uneven breath and continued, 'It's a big step to take, and I don't want to do anything I will later regret.'

Mario poured some wine into both of their glasses. 'Take all the time you need,' he said. 'I will have Giovanna move your things into my room after dinner.'

Her eyes flared. 'You want me to move into your room *straight away*?'

'That is what husbands and wives do, is it not?' he asked. 'Sharing a room and a bed are pretty standard, I would have thought.'

She swallowed and reached for one of the bread rolls Giovanna had left earlier, systematically crumbling it in her fingers without actually eating any of it.

'Would you like some butter or olive oil with your crumbs?' he asked drily.

She looked down at her plate and grimaced. 'Sorry…'

He smiled as he picked up his wine glass. 'I am not sure why I make you so nervous, *cara*—especially now that we have consummated our relationship. Believe me, it will only get better from now on.'

Sabrina knew she was blushing again but there was little she could do about it. He made her feel hot all over just by looking at her. The thought of experiencing more of his sensual expertise made her stomach dip and dive in excitement. When she squeezed her legs together she could feel where he had been earlier.

Giovanna came in with their entrée, and Mario instructed her to transfer Sabrina's things into his room before she left for the evening. The housekeeper gave Sabrina a twinkling look as she moved past to leave, making Sabrina's cheeks flame all over again.

'Now that is one very happy housekeeper,' Mario commented.

'Yes, well, one room is easier for her to clean than two,' Sabrina said.

'She has taken rather a shine to you, has she not?'

'No thanks to you,' she said with a sour set to her mouth. 'She was absolutely awful to me when I first arrived.'

A frown appeared between his eyes. 'You think I deliberately set her against you?'

She gave him an arch look. 'Didn't you?'

'Of course not,' he said, still frowning. 'Perhaps she read something in the press. I will have a word with her about it.'

'There's no need to do that,' Sabrina inserted quickly. 'Whatever she heard or read, she has obviously disregarded. She is lovely towards me now, and she adores Molly.'

'Giovanna has been in the service of my family for a long time,' he said. 'I know for a fact she is delighted I have finally settled down.'

'You don't strike me as the tameable, settling-down type,' Sabrina said as she picked up her spoon.

The smile fell away from his face as he reached for his glass. 'Perhaps I will change,' he said, swirling the red wine for a moment. He met her eyes once more and added, 'But don't hold your breath.'

She gave him an 'I wouldn't be so foolish' look. 'Believe me, I wasn't going to.'

Once the meal was over, Mario led her into the salon for a liqueur. He turned on the sound system; the strains of a mellow-sounding ballad made Sabrina's nervous tension gradually fade away. She laid her head back on the cushioned sofa, closing her eyes as the sweet cadences floated over her.

She felt the depression on the seat next to her as Mario joined her. The strong band of his arm lay on the back of the sofa, his fingers idly playing with her hair at the nape of her neck. She suppressed a tiny shiver of delight as he loosened the clip holding her hair up, the tresses falling down over his hand.

'You have beautiful hair,' he said in a throaty tone. 'Promise me you won't cut it.'

Sabrina turned her head to look at him. She felt ready to promise him just about anything when he looked at her like that. His eyes were dark and intense, his mouth so close she could see every pinpoint of stubble around its sensual curve. Almost without realising she was doing it, she raised her hand and gently traced over the sculptured contours of his lips, her belly giving a little, punching-fist-like movement as his tongue came out and brushed over her fingertip.

'Kiss me, Sabrina.'

She leaned towards him, her eyelids going down as she felt the gentle breeze of his breath caress her lips. She pressed her mouth to his, softly, hesitantly, tasting him, feeling the simmer of sexual heat spring fervently to boiling life.

He took over the kiss with a sweep of his tongue across the seam of her mouth, taking possession of her moist warmth, calling her tongue into a Latino salsa that was smoulderingly sexy. Sparks of reaction raced up and down her spine as his hands brought her nearer, one hand splayed at the back of her head, the other cupping the swell of her breast. She pressed herself closer as his thumb found her nipple, teasing it until it ached for the intimate caress of his mouth.

Her body throbbed with an insistent pulse, an on-off rhythm that resounded deep in her womb. Moisture pooled between her thighs, the humidity of need that would not be denied now it had been awakened. She felt the raw ache consume her as she strained to get closer to him; she ached to feel the power of him under her touch.

She groped blindly for his shirt buttons as his mouth continued its passionate command of hers, undoing each one until her hands found his warm, hard flesh. She moved lower, undoing his belt and unhooking his waistband, rolling down his zip until she took him in her hand.

He broke the kiss to watch her caress him, his breathing becoming deep and uneven. 'Harder, *cara*—don't be frightened to use more pressure. I like it that way.'

Sabrina made a circle with her fingers and massaged him, taking her cue from his reaction. He sucked in a breath, his jaw clenched as he fought to keep his head, pleasure written all over his features. He beaded with moisture, and she bent her head and tasted him, delighting in the way he quivered against her mouth. She licked him again, using her tongue to tantalise him, to string out the pleasure. She could feel the tension building in him with every smooth stroke of her tongue.

'Enough,' he groaned as he pulled away. He took a couple of deep breaths and then began to work on her clothes. 'Let's even the score, shall we?'

Sabrina tried to control her frantic breathing as he slowly undressed her. Each item of clothing was taken from her body with a series of burning kisses that branded her flesh, sending an electric current of need to her inner core. She lay back on the sofa as he came over her, his mouth sucking on her breast as his fingers explored the moist heart of her. The stroking motion stirred her senses into a frenzy; she arched her back, striving for the ultimate moment, hovering precariously on the edge, not quite there, but so close she could feel every nerve tensing and twitching.

His mouth left her breast to kiss its way down her body, lingering over the tiny bowl of her belly button before going lower. Sabrina snatched in a sharp breath as his lips nibbled at the sensitive curve of each of her hips, a tiny, teasing nip that made every nerve beneath the skin leap in awareness.

'You have such silky, creamy skin,' he said as he began to trace her inner thighs with his fingers in a lazy 'I've got all the time in the world' motion that made her nearly scream out loud in frustration. 'It is like satin; so smooth and warm. I want to taste every inch of you.'

Her heart rate soared as his fingers moved closer, milli-metre by millimetre, the tight coil of tension in her body threatening to snap. She gasped when he separated her, the gentle caress making her quiver all over in pleasure.

'You are so slick and warm, so ready for me,' he said as he continued stroking her.

'I want you inside…' she said in a breathy whisper.

'It's probably too soon after the last time,' he said. 'You are new to this, *cara*. Your body will be tender. Let me plea-sure you this way.'

Sabrina grasped his hand, her eyes pleading. 'No, please, Mario. I want you to make love to me. I want to feel you again.'

He held her gaze for a moment before he lowered his mouth to hers, kissing her until she was writhing with longing.

He reached for where he had thrown his trousers, and, taking out his wallet, retrieved a tiny square that contained a condom. He quickly applied it before coming down over her, positioning himself so she wasn't taking all of his weight.

His first thrust was gentle, making Sabrina's skin leap in excitement, a rush of feeling so intense it took her breath away.

'Am I hurting you?' Mario asked, tensing.

She let out a sigh of bliss. 'No, it's perfect. You are perfect.'

Mario gradually increased his pace, becoming lost in the sensations flooding his system. She was such a generous lover, so willing to give as well as receive. He was blown away by the power her body had over him. Making love with her was so different from his other experiences. She somehow lifted him to another sphere, a place where mind, body and soul were inextricably linked, where feelings he had not thought possible began to unfurl inside him like a tight bud blossoming under the first rays of warm spring sun.

He loved the way her body fit his as if it had been especially for him. Her slim limbs wrapped around him so naturally; her soft mouth received his with such warmth, and her feminine heart gripped him as if she never wanted to let him go.

Mario felt her shudder as he drove a little harder, her body starting to convulse around his as she came. He felt a powerful surge of emotion as she gasped and whimpered his name, her slender arms holding him tightly as the tumult of her orgasm ricocheted through her. His own release was just as powerful; it bulleted through him like a pump-action rifle, sending him tumbling in a vortex of sensation that was totally earth-shattering.

Mario lay with her encircled in his arms as their heart

rates gradually returned to normal, his fingers idly playing a rhythmic tune on the silky skin of her arm as if on a keyboard. It wasn't a song he recognised—it had no words—but he knew he didn't want it to end.

Not yet.

CHAPTER ELEVEN

THE baby monitor sounded and Sabrina moved out of Mario's arms, retrieving her clothes from the flaoor, trying not to feel embarrassed at her nakedness. 'I'd better go and see if she needs changing or something,' she said as she dressed with as much dignity as she could.

Mario seemed less concerned about his lack of covering. He sat upright and brushed his hair back with his hand. 'I'll come with you,' he said, and reached for his trousers.

Sabrina's eyes fell away from his. She was annoyed with herself for feeling ashamed of the intimacy they had shared. It made her seem so unsophisticated and homely. 'Don't worry,' she said. 'It might wake her up too much to have both of us fussing over her.'

'As you wish.'

Sabrina didn't let out her breath until she was in the nursery tending to the baby's needs. Molly was soon resettled, and Sabrina tiptoed out, leaving the door ajar.

She was on her way back from a visit to the bathroom when she heard Mario talking to someone. At first she thought it must be Giovanna, but then she realised he was speaking on the phone in the master bedroom, as she could only hear his side of the conversation. She had always loathed people who eavesdropped, but something about the tone of his voice stopped her in her tracks just outside the door. Although he was speaking in Italian, she heard her name mentioned a couple of times, the urgency in his voice making her wonder who exactly he was talking to. When she considered the possibility of him discussing her with another woman, after the intimacy they had so recently shared, her heart began to pound like a pendulum that had been knocked out of kilter, each strike against her chest-wall making her feel as if her fragile hopes were being bludgeoned one by one.

Sabrina was not aware of making a sound, but suddenly Mario pulled the bedroom door fully open, the mobile in his hand now flipped closed. His mouth was pulled tight, his jaw even tighter. 'I am sorry about this, Sabrina, but I have to go out for a while,' he said, his eyes moving out of range of hers. 'I might not be back until late.'

She frowned as he snatched his car keys off the bedside table, his hand going through his hair once more. 'Mario?'

His eyes cut to hers. 'Leave it, Sabrina,' he said, his tone edgy. 'We will talk in the morning. I have to get going. Someone is waiting for me.'

She opened her mouth, but closed it again as he brushed past. Her shoulders went down, her spirits plummeting in despair.

Someone was waiting for him.

The words taunted her as each minute of each hour dragged past, as she lay listening in vain for Mario's return.

It was the longest and loneliest night of her life.

* * *

When Sabrina came downstairs the next morning, bleary-eyed and with a pounding headache, she saw Giovanna start as she entered the kitchen, the newspaper she had been reading hastily snatched out of sight.

'*La prima colazione*, Signora Marcolini?' she asked, wiping her hands on her apron.

Sabrina lifted her hands in a gesture of helplessness. 'I'm sorry, Giovanna. Can you say it in English, please?'

'Breakfast,' the housekeeper said, not quite meeting Sabrina's gaze. 'I have some fresh rolls and preserves, or if you like I have cured ham and cheese, and—'

'It's all right, Giovanna,' she said with a sigh. 'I am not feeling like food just now.'

'Did the *bambino* keep you awake last night?' Giovanna asked as she surreptitiously put the newspaper in the bin under the sink.

'She only woke once, and only briefly,' Sabrina said, peering past the housekeeper's shoulder to the bin. 'Is that today's paper?'

Giovanna pursed her lips for a moment. 'You not able to read it, *signora*. It is in Italian.'

It suddenly became absolutely imperative for Sabrina to see it. She moved past Giovanna and pulled the scrunched-up paper out of the bin, smoothing it out to see the front page. Looking at the photograph of Mario and a blonde woman draped all over him made her chest feel as if someone had kicked her whilst wearing a concrete boot. She swallowed tightly, trying to control her emotions. 'What does it say, Giovanna?' she asked, lowering the paper to look at the housekeeper.

Giovanna lifted her apron to wipe the beads of perspiration

off her face. 'It say…' she gave Sabrina a wincing look '…it say Mario Marcolini resumes affair with Glenda Rickman.'

Sabrina swallowed again, her throat feeling razor-blade raw. 'Glenda Rickman the model?'

Giovanna nodded grimly. 'She was his mistress before he married you.'

Sabrina drew in a breath that burned all the way down into her lungs. 'I see…'

'I told you before, lots of rich Italian men have mistresses,' Giovanna said. 'You are his wife. That is all that matters.'

Sabrina closed the paper and handed it back to the house-keeper. 'When—or should I say *if*—Signore Marcolini comes home some time today, I would like you to inform him I am taking Molly with me for a few days to think over his offer.'

Giovanna frowned uncertainly. '*Sì?*'

Sabrina straightened her spine in resolve. 'I want some time to consider my options,' she said. 'I am not sure I am cut out for the life he expects me to live here with him.'

Giovanna began to wring her hands. 'You must not go where he cannot find you, Signora Marcolini,' she insisted. 'He will be very angry.'

Sabrina remained implacable and calm, although inside she felt cut to ribbons. 'Let him be angry,' she said. 'I am angry too. We can't go on like this without some give on his part.'

'He give you diamonds!' Giovanna threw her hands in the air. 'He give you a *palazzo* and expensive clothes. He treat you like a *principessa*—how you say in English?—a princess. You are his wife, *signora*. You share his bed.'

Sabrina felt her bottom lip quiver as tears came to her eyes. 'I don't want his priceless diamonds and his stupid designer-clothes.'

Giovanna looked confused. 'What do you want from him?'

I want his heart, Sabrina said, but not out loud. 'Tell him I will call him in three days,' she said. 'My mobile will be switched off until then.'

Mario slammed his fist on the kitchen counter as he grilled the housekeeper for the umpteenth time. 'What do you mean, she has taken Molly away?' he roared. 'Where the hell is she? She *must* have told you where she was going.'

Giovanna flinched, blinking back tears. 'I tell her not to go, but she not listen to me. She not tell me anything about where she was going. She called a cab and was gone before I could contact you.'

Mario swore viciously as he left the room, pacing up and down, trying to think where Sabrina could possibly have gone. She had money and she had Molly. She could be on a plane to anywhere by now.

His chest tightened at the thought of something happening to either of them. He wasn't used to feeling so utterly powerless. How had he not foreseen this? He had trusted Sabrina too much. He had thought she had been softening towards him; each day he had felt her move closer to him, letting her guard down. God damn it, she had given herself to him, fooling him into believing she might be developing feelings for him, when all the time she was planning an escape route. He suddenly recalled how he had overheard her telling Molly she was going to think of a way out of the situation on the day of the funeral.

All this time—he clenched his teeth until they almost cracked—*all this time* she had been planning a revenge so complete it would destroy him. If the press heard of it he would look a complete fool. He could handle that, but he could not handle Sabrina deserting him just when he had begun to realise how much he needed her. It wasn't just about Molly; perhaps it had never been about Molly. From the first moment he had met Sabrina he had felt strangely unsatisfied, felt an irksome feeling that something was missing from his life, but until now he hadn't been able to identify exactly what it was.

. The *palazzo* was so achingly empty. Had it always been that way? Why hadn't he noticed it before? His footsteps echoed ominously throughout the corridors as he searched every room again and again, looking for some clue as to where Sabrina had gone.

The nursery smelt of baby powder, and Mario felt his insides clench as he picked up a tiny pink all-in-one baby suit. His fingers tightened around it, thinking of the pain his brother must have gone through when his tiny daughter had been stillborn.

He loosened his grip on the little suit, its softness slipping through his fingers as he laid it gently back down on the dresser. He swallowed a thick lump of emotion as he thought about Antonio being brave enough to take on the prospect of another child with the woman he had loved enough to put his life on pause for for five long, lonely years.

Mario felt ashamed of how shallow and selfish he had become. Antonio had been rather blunt about it last night before they'd been rudely interrupted by both the press and Mario's playboy past. Mario could see now it was no wonder Sabrina had baulked at his plan for a loveless, childless marriage. Children were everything to her. She lived to look after and nurture others. He had seen her grey eyes light up whenever she looked at Molly. But he had denied her the dream of having her own child, blackmailing her into a relationship that gave her money and jewels and prestige, but not the thing she most desired.

'Signore Marcolini?' Giovanna spoke tentatively from the door.

He turned and faced her, stripping his face of emotion. *'Sì?'*

'The dinner tonight…' she said, pausing as if waiting for the fall out. 'I have pressed your suit for you.'

Mario swore as he glanced at his watch. 'Call my brother and tell him I can't make it,' he instructed Giovanna as he strode out of the nursery towards his study to check his computer. 'He'll understand. Tell him I have decided I have other things to see to that are far more important.'

Sabrina sat on the sunny terrace with Molly asleep in her pram just inside the doors, where she could hear her if she stirred. The villa she had rented at Positano was small but perfectly placed so she could have the peace and quiet she needed to face the biggest decision of her life.

She had read of the village in an Internet tour-guide and had felt immediately drawn to it. It was a haven-like place, or so the guide had said. It was protected from the winds by the Lattari Mountains, the dry, mild climate attracting tourists all year round. The guide had also pointed out that the author John Steinbeck had once written in an essay published in the 1950's:

Positano bites deep. It is a dream place that isn't quite real when you are there, and becomes beckoningly real after you are gone.

Those words seemed hauntingly relevant to Sabrina's relationship with Mario. Her love for him had bitten deep; she felt the teeth marks of it in her soul.

Their marriage wasn't real—more hauntingly familiar words—but now she was gone it seemed very real indeed. Could she walk away from Molly and leave Mario to his life of luxury and freedom? Or could she stay and shelve her hopes for a family of her own to make that ultimate sacrifice for him?

In the end it was not such a hard decision to make. She had been away from him just one day and she knew if he was standing here right now what she would say.

Sabrina looked up in surprise when she heard the sound of footsteps on the terrace. Her heart knocked against her ribcage when she saw Mario standing there, looking down at her.

'Next time you want to cover your tracks, *cara*,' he said in an unreadable tone, 'It might be an idea to delete all the sites you have been surfing on the Internet.'

She got up from the sun lounger on unsteady legs. 'Mario, I…I have something to say to you.'

He thrust his hands deep into his trouser pockets as if he was worried he might use them inappropriately. He looked haggard, drawn and hollow under the eyes, as if he had not slept. She took a step towards him, but he set his mouth and turned his back to look at the ocean below.

His voice when he spoke sounded empty; it echoed with regret. 'I don't blame you, Sabrina.'

Sabrina flicked her tongue across her lips, waiting for him to go on.

He stood there a moment or two before he turned back to face her, his expression rueful but composed.

'I don't blame you for leaving me,' he said. 'It is what I deserve for how I have treated you from the start.'

She stood very still, barely moving her chest up and down to breathe.

'I have been a fool,' he continued. 'It was only after you left that I realised how much of a fool I have been.'

Sabrina suddenly realised what it would be like. Year after year it would be exactly like this—him coming to apologise for yet another indiscretion, a little fling that the press had got wind of and run in the next day's paper to spread her shame at not being able to keep him happy at home. He would apologise, she would forgive him and the hurt would eat away at her until there was nothing left.

Anger bubbled up inside her—anger at how she had fallen for him when she had always known it would end like this, with her shattered while he was barely affected. She clenched her hands into tight balls of resentment, her voice coming out higher and shriller than she had expected as her emotions got the better of her. 'Why did you have to sleep with me?' she choked over the words. 'Why did you have to turn me into yet another one of your cheap bedmates? *Why?*'

Mario took her tightly clenched hands in his, holding them securely as he looked down at her flushed face. 'Sabrina, you are not listening to me. Stop shouting at me for a moment and let me tell you what I came here to say.'

'Did you do it deliberately?' She flashed grey lightning at him with her eyes. 'Did you make me fall in love with you for a laugh? Were you laughing about me to *her*?'

'*Cara…*' Mario swallowed to clear the emotion that had surged up from deep inside him at her words. *She loved him.* It hardly seemed possible given what he had done.

'Why?' she asked again, her eyes now glistening with tears as she struggled to get out of his hold. 'Why did you sleep with me? Did you have to take it that far?'

Mario tightened his hold. 'I slept with you, *mio piccolo*, because I could not resist you. I slept with you because I wanted you to be mine.' He took a deep breath and added, 'I slept with you because I've fallen in love with you.'

Sabrina went slack in his grip. 'But…but you can't love me. The paper said you've gone back to your mistress. That was who you went to see the night before last, wasn't it?'

His expression darkened. 'I met with my brother. We met in one of our favourite bars, but we were interrupted by the arrival of Glenda and, of course, the press. She is insanely jealous I married you so soon after I ended things with her. She has never been rejected before, and decided to orchestrate a little payback.'

Sabrina bit her lip until it hurt. 'But the photo?'

'I know it looks incriminating, but the press always play on that sort of shot,' he said. 'I had just told her to stay away from me and my loved ones—in particular you—and she threw herself at me. What the press failed to report is that a few minutes later Security hauled her out of the building with the threat of an assault charge ringing in her ears.'

Sabrina looked into his dark eyes, her heart shifting in her chest as she saw how meltingly soft they were. 'You're not just saying it, are you? I mean, about the being in love part…?'

He wrapped his arms around her, bringing her close. 'I only realised it last night as I was talking to my brother,' he said. 'I was asking his advice on what to do about our situation. But while we were talking it made me think back over the last year or two since we first met at Ric and Laura's wedding, and then again at the christening. I started to see it then—how I had always been drawn to you. I couldn't get you out of my mind. I guess I was always a little bit in love with you. I think Ric and Laura sensed it too.'

She gave him a sheepish look from beneath her lashes as she confessed, 'I think I was always a little bit in love with you too.'

His hands came up to tenderly cup her face, his eyes centred on hers. 'Just a little bit in love?' he asked with a twinkling smile.

She beamed back at him radiantly. 'A big bit in love,' she said. 'Totally, irrevocably and immeasurably in love.'

'So will you marry me, Sabrina?' he asked.

She frowned at him in puzzlement. 'But, darling, we *are* already married.' She held up her hand to show him her wedding and engagement ring. 'See?'

'I mean a real wedding, *tesore mio*,' he said, looking even more serious now. 'I want to see you walk down the aisle towards me. I want to see you dressed in a beautiful white dress and long, trailing veil. I want to give you the best honeymoon you can dream of.' He paused for a second and added in a deeper, gruffer tone, 'And I want to give you a baby, maybe two.'

Her eyes opened wide. 'You're serious? Are you sure?'

He nodded and gripped her hands tightly in his. 'It took a few lonely hours without you and Molly to make me realise what I was throwing away. I want it all, Sabrina. I want you and Molly and a family of our own.'

She nestled closer, and linking her arms around his neck, pressed a soft kiss to his mouth. 'I love you,' she said. 'I love you so much, I was planning on telling you when I got back that I would stay with you, children or no children.'

Mario held her from him, looking into her grey eyes, feeling a sense of completeness he had never dreamed possible. 'You are the most giving and loving person I have ever met. What did I do to deserve you?'

She sighed and hugged him tight, her head pressed against his heart. 'I can't believe this is happening I was so miserable when I thought you were seeing someone else.'

Mario eased her away from him to look down at her again, his expression sombre. '*Cara*, it is always going to be like it was the other night—the press, I mean. They make money out of people like Antonio and I, making up scandals, speculating on our movements all the time. I need you to trust me otherwise it will destroy us as it very nearly destroyed him and Claire.'

Sabrina held his sincere gaze with love shining in her eyes. 'I do trust you, Mario. Ric and Laura trusted you. Molly trusts you. I think you are the most trustworthy and loyal man I've ever met.'

He kissed her softly. 'Thank you for saying that. It means the world to me. I never thought I would find someone like you. In fact, I didn't think people like you existed anymore. I thought my brother had found the last one.'

'About that honeymoon you spoke of,' Sabrina said smiling as she rubbed up against him like a sinuous cat against a pole. 'Do we have to wait until we get married for real?'

He scooped her up in his arms, his dark eyes glinting back at her sparkling ones. 'Who said anything about waiting? We're married, right?'

Sabrina smiled a blissful smile, hugging her arms tightly around his neck. 'Right,' she said.

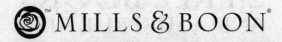

2 FREE BOOKS
AND A SURPRISE GIFT

We would like to take this opportunity to thank you for reading this Mills & Boon® book by offering you the chance to take TWO more specially selected titles from the Modern™ series absolutely FREE! We're also making this offer to introduce you to the benefits of the Mills & Boon® Book Club™—

- **FREE home delivery**
- **FREE gifts and competitions**
- **FREE monthly Newsletter**
- **Exclusive Mills & Boon Book Club offers**
- **Books available before they're in the shops**

Accepting these FREE books and gift places you under no obligation to buy, you may cancel at any time, even after receiving your free books. Simply complete your details below and return the entire page to the address below. You don't even need a stamp!

YES Please send me 2 free Modern books and a surprise gift. I understand that unless you hear from me, I will receive 4 superb new titles every month for just £3.19 each, postage and packing free. I am under no obligation to purchase any books and may cancel my subscription at any time. The free books and gift will be mine to keep in any case.

Ms/Mrs/Miss/Mr_____ initials _____

_____

Surname _____
address _____

_____
_____ postcode _____

Send this whole page to: Mills & Boon Book Club, Free Book Offer, FREEPOST NAT 10298, Richmond, TW9 1BR.